TALES OF SURVIVAL
in
COLONIAL
NEW ENGLAND

TALES OF SURVIVAL
in
COLONIAL
NEW ENGLAND

Connie Evans

Also by Connie Evans:

Ebenezer Mudgett and the Pine Tree Riot

Table of Contents

REUBEN

and the

WITCH

Mrs. William Dustin, as has been told, was the great Witch of Weare. Of her it could be said:—She roamed the country far and near,

Bewitched the children and the peasants,
Dried up the cows, and lamed the deer,
And sucked the eggs, and killed the pheasants.

—The History of Weare

Late summer, 1767

euben Favor was always on his best behavior when he knew the elders were watching him; his inner detection system had been well-honed over his short life. It had to be, to escape unscathed from the outcomes of the pranks he delighted in administering to his siblings. To avoid detection, he cultivated and perfected a smile, replete with moony eyes and a cock of his head that feigned adoration for his mother, which she breathed in as if he alone gave her the strength to live. She believed Reuben to be irreproachable, more perfect than any ten-year old boy could possibly be. His father was harder to impress. Realizing that his father did not fall prey to such manipulation, he simply stayed out of his way.

Reuben used his invisibility to his advantage when extra hands were needed around the homestead. Also, he learned early on that tattling on his four older brothers to defend his honor did not win respect or attention from his father; therefore, he maintained his silence and endured the humiliation of occasional black eyes and dirt-covered breeches and took solace in planning his revenge. His brothers had not learned that lesson. Their whining and complaints were always met with annoyance and a dismissive wave—if not a smack—of their father's hand.

Reuben soon calculated that performing his chores without the standard whining or dirt-kicking habit of his brothers and sisters would inevitably ensure his mother's praise. However, the oldest brothers, John and Joseph, considered the compliments she bestowed upon Reuben in their midst to be license for his mistreatment. They endeavored without end, or success, to reveal Reuben's true character, thereby hoping to exonerate themselves from all past, present, and future denunciations. The only problem with this theory was that Reuben was far smarter than the two hitched together, or even four of the oldest brothers, John, Joseph, Moses, and Cutting, amassed. He learned to subvert their intentions, or if that failed, to pay them back in spades. They simply were no match for him, but that never stopped them from trying.

During this time of year, the sun's presence was getting noticeably shorter, with enough nip in the evening air to encourage the females in the family to don their shawls. John, Joseph, and Mr. Favor had chopped and split enough firewood to challenge the impending daily battles against the brisk winter air, but they still needed to gather plenty of kindling to add to the dried corn husks. Reuben knew that sooner or later his mother would ask him to venture out into the woods to collect sticks and small branches. He was sitting on the split-rail fence, deep in thought, pondering whether to wait to be asked to perform the chore, at which time he would feign extreme cheerfulness to begin it, or to suddenly announce that he felt it his obligation to do it. He imagined that either way, both would end with his mother cupping his chin and looking lovingly into his eyes. He could endure that as long as one or more of his brothers were present. His plumpness did not prevent him from gracefully jumping off the fence and giving a little hop after landing. He headed toward the house.

John, tall and lanky, appeared from the back of the house and was taking long strides toward Reuben. Right behind him, trying to keep up, was freckle-faced Joseph. Upon approaching their younger brother, their eyes narrowed and smiled in an evil fashion. Their intentions were as clear in their expressions as if they had shouted them: Reuben knew he was the target. Joseph walked past Reuben. John stood in front, blocking Reuben's passage. The older boy stood with a wide stance, arms crossed, and a sneer spreading on his thin face.

"Where you goin', Rube?" The question sounded more like a threat.

Reuben had compiled a mental inventory of retorts and insults and was about to harvest a choice one. Smirking, he said, "I thought I'd let Mama know you were kissin' Abigail Parker behind the oak tree after school. Might her father be interested to know as well?"

Reuben knew John was sweet on Abigail and guessed that a kiss was a strong possibility. More than once he had seen the two of them together all sicky-eyed; each time he wanted to vomit. Reuben also fathomed that any mention of Abigail was sure to light John's short fuse. He was poised for the push he was certain was coming. *Otherwise, why was dim-witted Joseph positioned on all fours behind him?*

Reuben waited until he recognized the moment the fuse made headway into John's frail brain. John pressed his lips together, squinted his eyes, and raised his hands to grab him. Reuben hopped deftly to the side. John, not meeting any resistance, fell forward and toppled over Joseph. *Perfect timing again!* Reuben mentally congratulated himself but had learned long ago that total success depended on a quick getaway. As tempting as it was, he couldn't luxuriate on their looks of surprise and fury. He scurried away, leaving his brothers knotted up and swearing on the ground.

He scampered to the house and found his mother setting up the spinning jenny to weave their linen. He announced he was going to gather kindling, and she rewarded him with tender words and a smile. He darted out the back door to be sure to avoid his feral-looking brothers. He slithered through the vegetable garden among the potato plants and tall corn stalks to the barn, where he grabbed the large gathering sack.

He concluded that taking the longer route to the

woods, by hugging the edge of the hayfield, would be safer than venturing down the middle, but that did not stop him from looking anxiously in the direction of the house. He could not dismiss the notion that the Feeble Four, as he liked to call them, could appear at any moment running through the field and waving weapons of their own making. *Aye, the edge was a better choice.* Moses and Cutting, the closest in age to Reuben, would like nothing more than an excuse to tattle on Reuben.

Reuben darted unnoticed into the thick woods. He weaved his way around the giant tree trunks much like a field mouse twisted and turned through tall stalks of grass. He could enjoy the solitude of the forest more if the low vegetation didn't grab at his stockings. More than once he had to untangle himself from the prickers or burrs. His mother required that as soon as they could manage a needle and thread, each child had to repair their tears and pulls. It was the only pair he would have for a long while, and he did not relish mending them.

Several tenacious burrs clung to his waistcoat by the time the gathering cloth was full. He picked off the ones he could see and spun around in an attempt to determine the location of his house; it was easy to get confounded in the maze of pines, oaks, and birches. A screeching sound from above startled him. He emitted a nervous snigger when he realized it was simply two branches rubbing together. He snaked around a large granite boulder. *Is it a bit brighter to my right?* he thought. He maintained his sight on what could be a clearing. At last, rays of sunlight streamed through the trees. After scrambling up a steep hill while dragging his bulky load and yanking it free from the clutches of the numerous prickers, Reuben finally arrived on a road.

Sweat glistened on his brow. Reuben hoisted the sack over his shoulder again, the sticks poking him in his back. He staggered and then stopped to readjust the load when he noticed an approaching figure in the distance. Whoever it was did not walk with the purposeful steps of a brother seeking revenge. Also, it was clear by the clothing that the person was a woman. His brothers would try anything to get back at him, but they definitely would not go so far as to climb into their mother's skirts.

As she came closer, he was able to discern her features. *Mistress Dustin. The witch!* Reuben scanned the woods on both sides of the road in search of an escape. The trees and underbrush had become too tightly packed for him to slip in with his cumbersome sack. When he turned back to look up the road, it seemed that she had advanced much too quickly, as if she had glided closer while his back was turned. The wind picked up. Leaves fluttered and swirled around him. *So many leaves, all so suddenly.* Mistress Dustin was getting nearer; he could see she was carrying something in a basket. *Surely something to cause me harm.* He was fixated on the basket when she spoke.

"Good day, young sir!"

Her cheerfulness made him wary. He side-stepped closer to the wall of trees, tripping over a rock but managing to remain upright. Her shawl and skirts billowed and whipped. *She's going to take flight any second.* His mouth hung open and his eyes widened. *Any second . . . any second . . .*

"Close your mouth, Reuben," she said, not slowing her step, "Pray, you do not want to catch a fly." Her eyes crinkled into a smile as she passed.

She winked at me!

Reuben snapped his mouth shut so quickly his teeth clattered. He stood motionless and transfixed to the earth until she was well past him, and then he began to run. His gait was awkward; his right arm was caught behind him to drag the sack, and his left hand pressed against his pounding heart to keep it inside his chest. Without the use of his arms to pump, his feet could not gain sufficient purchase. *I can sense her slowin' me down!*

Reuben recalled Joseph's story from the other day that Mistress Dustin had already changed boys like himself into a whole diversity of animals; the thought of snuffling around like a hog searching for food was enough to release his hand from his chest and pump his arm as fast as his father's sawing timber. When he thought it safe to turn around, he stopped and looked. She had vanished! Indeed, she could have turned beyond the curve. *More likely—she simply faded away!* Reuben felt a chill go down his back. His hand tightened on the sack and he started to run again.

Mistress Dustin did not have to hear the rumors. She was well aware that folks thought her a witch. She could tell by the wide berths and quickened pace people made at passing. She endured the accusations of their animals' and families' afflictions and everything from crops failing to cream not turning to butter in her neighbors' churns. Rhoda Dustin suffered the effrontery and recriminations the best she could. There would be no use in trying to change the collective belief engraved in people's minds. No, she was *not* a witch; if anything, she was the town scapegoat.

Rhoda had endeavored to defend herself once. It was well before her first child was born. She was on her way to the Bailey's homestead intending to swap her eggs for a jug of milk. She was walking the path by the Bailey's cow pasture and humming her favorite hymn, *Blest Be the Tie That Binds*. Her heart swelled and rose in her chest from the sheer happiness she felt. It was a perfect summer's day, and she was out from under her parents' roof as a newly married woman! She was but a short distance from the Bailey's home when she could see a few members of the family bunched up at the pasture gate watching the cattle as they grazed. Rhoda stopped for a second to enjoy the antics of two curious calves nearby making awkward jumps.

A black form in the distance caught her attention. The cattle blocked the Baileys' view of it, but Rhoda was behind the cows and off to the left where she had a better vantage point. Suddenly, the cows began bawling and then bolted. The calves ran after their mothers with their tails in the air, a sure sign of fear. Rhoda saw the bear skirt around an outcropping of rocks and disappear; however, his presence and smell, undetected by the Baileys, had incited pandemonium among the cattle. The panicked cows stampeded around the pasture and worked themselves into a frenzy. Rhoda began to run toward the Baileys, afraid the cattle would break through the fence, which they did in short order. The Baileys scattered to look for grain buckets and ropes to retrieve their herd. Mr. Bailey halted when he saw Rhoda.

"By God's blood! Why did you do that?!"

Rhoda, stunned, stopped still. At first she thought he was funning her, but his furious expression did not ease up any before he dashed after his animals.

When they finally contained the cattle, Rhoda tried to explain what she had seen, a bear, but they had seen nothing of the sort. Mistress Bailey accused her of lying and having evil powers. The story of the spell she had cast on the cows to cause them to stampede when they were pleasantly grazing spread from neighbor to neighbor. She had pleaded with people that the bear was the culprit, but her explanation had no effect. The accusation was no different from her being branded by a hot iron—and hurt as deeply and marked her as indelibly. Henceforth the townspeople, including the Favors, labelled her a witch.

Rhoda was acquainted with the Favor family. Her children often had to defend themselves against the shenanigans of the oldest Favor boys. Certainly, the Favor boys had plenty of fodder with the Dustins' mother, believing, among other unworldly acts, that Mistress Dustin routinely walked upside down like an insect on the ceiling. Regardless of their opinion of her, the boys' bursts of animosity generally stemmed from the unspoken competition in school between the two sets of children, where the four Dustins mercilessly outmatched the Favors in intellect.

Reuben's older brothers stammered and stumbled reciting verses from the Bible while the Dustins stood erect and recited their verses flawlessly. The Favors were most often eliminated in the first round of the spelling bees, while the Dustins excelled, and the Favors could not master the art of using their quills without blotches of ink spreading over their misspelled words. During recess, outside and away from the schoolmaster's eyes, the Favors endeavored to equalize the score.

Reuben was an exception. Where his brothers failed miserably in school, he excelled. While they wrestled, he wandered off to engage in games of tag or snap the whip. Because Reuben was never the cause of the bruises and black eyes her children brought home from school, Mistress Dustin had no cause to dislike him.

Reuben arrived at the barn, after his encounter with Mistress Dustin, breathing hard and sweating in spite of the soft August breeze. He was annoyed with the woman. She had caused him to work up the sweat, and assuredly, the wink was some kind of spell she administered on him. He remained on his guard, listening for the telltale snickering of the Feeble Four or the constant rows and shoving between them. He dumped his sack of kindling in the wood bin, slung the empty cloth over the side of it, and went to his secret place in a dark corner of the barn. There was just enough room for his chubby body to squeeze between some discarded planks of oak and pine. The episode with Mistress Dustin had caused him much consternation, and he needed to rest.

The sudden recognition of voices startled him. Judging by the sounds and complaining, he realized that his older brothers were fetching pitchforks and long poles. He had witnessed his father taking the scythe to the field after breakfast; by now he had cut enough of a swath that he required others to get the hay to the barn. *The best thing I can do now is be still. Otherwise, I'll be spendin' my afternoon chuckin' hay.* His brothers were too busy grumbling and swearing to hear any noise that could divulge Reuben's whereabouts.

When enough time had passed, Reuben snuck toward the house. As he walked, he took a hasty glance around the immediate property. He shielded his eyes from the sun and grinned as he noticed the activity in the hayfield. His brothers were pitching the final hay cut onto the long poles that they would then have to drag into the barn. *I'm not sorry that I missed father's call to help with that dusty, itchy chore; soon I'll be as safe as a rabbit in a den.* He began to skip.

His sister, Betsey, was sitting on the step in front of the door, her small hands struggling to tie unwieldy hemlock boughs to broom poles. She stamped her feet and let out a frustrated growl.

"I cannot do it!"

"Why bother yourself, you shan't be able to get them fastened tight enough. You shall never manage to sweep with that pitiful broom," Reuben scoffed.

"Reuben, put your finger here so I can tie the knot," Betsey mumbled, while holding the end of a fibrous strand of hemp between her teeth.

"'Tis of trifling importance to me at present. I have more urgent affairs," he sniffed.

She spit the hemp out of her mouth, "Reuben! 'Twill take but a moment!"

Reuben ignored her. He climbed the next step, making sure he knocked against Betsey. She yelped and attempted to push back, but he hopped out of her way. Smirking, he opened the door. He caught a glimpse of his mother approaching to check on Betsey's progress. Her head was down and she was wiping her hands on a cloth tied around her middle. He backed down a step and paused. He waited until he was sure his mother was within earshot. Just to be certain, he cleared his throat and raised his voice. He turned to Betsey.

"Dear Sister, let me help you. Indeed, it must be difficult with such small fingers."

Betsey gave him a puzzled look. Then she looked behind him and saw their mother leaning against the doorframe, a proud smile stretched across her tired face. Betsey pinched back one corner of her mouth and glared at Reuben through narrowed eyes before rolling them in disgust.

"Oh, that I had a brother so endearing when I was but a young girl," Mistress Favor sighed.

Reuben flashed his mother another one of his dewy-eyed smiles that would make any lickspittle envious. As he went through the doorway, she ruffled his blond hair. He wrinkled his nose after passing her.

Once inside, he strolled into their sparse cooking area. No one had followed him, and he seized on the opportunity of finding himself alone. Opening the tin cylinder candle box pegged to the wall, he snatched the flint. He stuffed it into the pocket he had begged his mother to sew into his breeches. A moment later she entered carrying the baby, Polly. He sensed her presence and casually turned around.

"Are you enjoying the bright sunshine of this day, Mother? I most certainly am—in spite of laboring to carry my *heavy* load of kindlin' through the *dark* woods and . . ."

"Pray, return out of doors to bask in its warmth and help your brothers with the haying, Reuben." She said, gently placing Polly in the pine-box cradle. Her little head of curls swayed side to side while she drifted off to sleep.

Meanwhile, Reuben's sharp mind went into action. He had no intention of joining his brothers.

"Mother, I was just fixing to tell you that I saw Mistress Dustin when returning with the kindlin'. She gave me a terrible, *evil* look; I was unable to budge. I stood transfixed for quite a time. She *winked* at me! I remain unrecovered from the event. I believe my insides are scrambled." He screwed up his face, bent at the waist, and gripped his stomach.

Mistress Favor took Reuben by his soft, plump shoulders and leaned forward to study his wide-set, cornflower blue eyes, as if trying to look through them all the way to his innards. Unable to discern any slight irregularity, she released one shoulder and swept the blond strands from his forehead.

"Oh Reuben, your forehead is damp. Perhaps you should lie down a bit. I'll fetch you some cider."

She disappeared into the cellar. Reuben sat down on the stool near her spinning jenny. He gave the wheel a spin, the thread twisting on the spindle fascinated him. When he heard her footsteps, he immediately stopped the wheel and slumped. He put his hands to his temples and groaned. Since the incident with Mistress Dustin was distressing his mother, he decided to use it to his advantage.

"Oh Mother, I fear I have damaged my stockings whilst gathering the sticks. I am feeling too wretched to repair them."

"No need to vex yourself; I can put aside some time this eve to mend them." She returned his sorrowful countenance with a sympathetic smile and worrisome sigh. She handed him a tin cup with the aromatic beverage. He drank it fast; a small rivulet ran down his chin.

"I shall fetch your bedroll and you can lie yourself down. I shall appraise your father of your condition."

With one arm wrapped around him, she pressed him against her meaty hip, nearly lifting him off the ground. Reuben fought the urge to twist free of his mother's iron grip, and the two ambled together to the next room. The toddler, Rebecca, was already curled up on her bedroll in the corner. She started to whimper and flutter her eyelids, firmly immersed in an upsetting dream. Mistress Favor released Reuben to yank down the bed secured against the wall of the sitting room and to grab his bedroll tucked inside. Then she stooped down to place a soothing hand on Rebecca's back, whose unconscious chewing motions showed she was still dreaming.

"Mother, 'tis been a while since I have found the time to stuff my bedding with fresh corn husks, and I fear I need all the comfort I can get at present. Pray, allow me to rest myself in your bed—just for a while?"

She blew a lock of wavy brown hair away from her face and tucked it back under her cap. "Of course, Reuben."

The bed sagged a bit from multiple bodies having stretched the ropes tied under the thin mattress. Rags and corn husks stuffed inside created mounds and valleys. Reuben had always preferred sleeping in his bedroll quite alone compared to suffering the jabbing elbows and kicking feet of any number of family members in the bed. This would be a treat to doze untouched in the big bed. He tried not to look too comfortable but returned his mother's concerned look with a weak smile.

She exhaled a deep breath and left him to resume her spinning; however, she could not release the worry from her brow. *Who knows the damage Mistress Dustin may have caused with her wink.*

Rhoda Dustin put her basket on the table and called to locate her husband, "William, I am returned!"

Although unintelligible, she heard his muffled voice coming from the woodshed. It was no surprise to see him in there stacking wood or near thereabouts splitting more. Until the end of April the fireplaces in their tavern would devour several loads of wood a day, but the fireplace in the kitchen would require the fuel year-round to cook. It was an interminable chore, demanding all members of the family to devote time and energy to the process. Her sons' laughter floated in the air above the harsh whacks and cracking sounds of dry-wood splitting.

"I see you have found some enjoyment in your work!" She smiled as she walked toward them.

William was mostly skin and bones, but his arms showed he was no stranger to swinging the axe. Her sons, Peter and Asa, carried the physical traits from her side of the family; they were stocky and already showed signs of strength. *They will be strapping and taller than their father for sure.*

"I got a good trade for the onions. Mistress Eastman had some lovely squash."

The Eastmans were just a few of the townspeople who turned a deaf ear to the witch rumors circling among the Weare homesteads—or else they feared not to participate in the bartering process that was essential among the neighbors. The early settlers depended on their small community for necessities they did not raise or grow.

Rhoda apparently interrupted a story Asa was sharing. Peter continued to stack the wood their father had split, but Asa was taking a break. He still had the glow in his eyes from telling one of his tales. William leaned on his axe, chuckling. Asa was the jovial one of the family. His cheerful attitude was infectious; one or two of his sisters often trailed after him, expecting to be entertained. All except Sarah. She was the oldest and maintained an edge of severity that perplexed her parents. While Asa brushed the witch rumors off with a joke, Sarah took them to heart. Rhoda worried that her beautiful, brown-eyed daughter believed them. She often caught Sarah staring at her as if she expected her mother to perform some otherworldly act.

"I met Reuben Favor on the road. I quite

frightened him, I believe. He seemed to think I was about to snatch him up!"

"'Twould be no loss if you had, Mother!" Peter laughed and looked at Asa.

"I s'pose he is the best of the lot—but we are not dealing with a good crop there!" Asa returned Peter's look and grinned with an accompanying nod.

"Still, I do wish the young ones would not be so fearful. They believe stories from their parents," she sighed.

Peter put his arm around his mother and whispered in her ear, "If they could just taste your indian pudding, you would surely turn 'em!"

Rhoda laughed and gave him a squeeze. "I would have to include a concoction they accuse me of making to turn 'em round!"

➶➶➶✕❰❰❰

Reuben faced the wall so his mother would not see the contentment on his face. He twisted and turned his chubby body into the mattress to push the lumps aside and make a comfortable cavity. Minutes later he was sound asleep, but the all-too-common noise of his brothers fighting outside the house interrupted his pleasant dream. He heard their father's boots stomping up the steps and thought he even heard him snort—the familiar sound of annoyance with his sons' scuffles.

Reuben dove off the bed and slammed it back against the wall, waking the toddler who commenced to cry. Reuben ran to the kitchen; his mother was humming in front of the fireplace and seemed occupied enough pushing the bean porridge around with a long-handled wooden spoon. She held the iron pot with a rag to prevent it from swinging and then pushed the long arm holding the pot off to the side. The beans bubbled and released a delicious fragrance in the small room.

Reuben grabbed a porridge paddle and knelt beside her on the long brick hearth. He uncovered the kettle on the opposite side of the beans with the rag his mother had used and began stirring the cornmeal mush. It had been simmering on the embers all day. She gave him one of her long and gripping hugs to acknowledge her appreciation before Rebecca waddled in and clutched and pulled at her skirts. Reuben sensed his father standing in the doorway. His brothers popped up from behind his bulky frame. Reuben exhaled a puff of breath through his nose but remained still except for his arm stirring the porridge.

Mistress Favor turned, dragging Rebecca as she faced her husband. She put her finger up to her lips to ward off the anger that was about to issue from her husband's mouth. She shooed him with her hands as she marched in their direction. Reuben peeked; he noted she was determined to plow into them if they did not back up into the sitting room. She left the young child detached from her skirts, huddled on the floor, but soon a black bug captured her attention. The toddler squealed in fascination as the bug scurried across the wood floor and dove between the planks.

Reuben stopped stirring. He heard his father growling about Reuben's disappearance just when he was needed to help with the haying. His mother tried to hush him, attempting to whisper an explanation. Reuben strained to interpret her muffled words over his brothers' incessant bellyaching and jumping up and down; they could not contain their grievance and frustration with Reuben. Suddenly there was a *thwack,* then another. The bellyaching turned to sniveling as the Feeble Four retreated outside. The sounds of their indignation faded away in the late summer air. From then on, Reuben could only divine individual words among his father's harrumphing, but he heard enough to discern that she was telling him about Mistress Dustin's wink.

Mr. Favor ambled into the room and studied Reuben. Reuben was accustomed to his father's interminable silent stares, attempting to induce babbling confessions. He had witnessed more than one brother yield under the pressure. Reuben fixed his eyes as if in a trance and maintained a steady stirring of the mush. Periodically, he squeezed the muscles in his neck and shoulders to dramatize a tremor or a tick. Finally, convinced that Mistress Dustin's wink maintained some lingering effect, his father left, frowning. He did not chastise Reuben for failing to join the haying.

Rhoda Dustin tried not to be impatient with Sarah. Granted, the process of making cloth was very long and tedious, but if she wanted to wear a dress that fit, she had better help with the labor. William and her sons had finished pulling, rotting, and breaking the flax. It was up to the women to take over and do the combing. Without their patch of flax they would have no sheets, towels, or clothing. This season produced a fair amount, which meant more than a fair amount of work to process it.

"Daughter, you are the fortunate one. Your sisters get your out-grown homespun whilst you get a new one." She tried to placate Sarah and draw a smile from her lips. "Besides, your father and brothers have the hard work. Once we finish with the combin' and removin' the tow you can prepare for the distaff, or Elizabeth can do the windin' 'round the spindle if you prefer."

"No, Mother. I shall do the windin' and Elizabeth can remove the tow."

Mistress Dustin hid her smile. By giving Sarah a choice, she had agreed to put at least some effort into one of the chores. Anyway, Elizabeth was more adept than Sarah at removing the coarse and broken part of the flax fibers. Nevertheless, they still had to weave it, then buck and belt it on a smooth, flat stone, wash the material, and spread it out on the grass or bushes to bleach in the sun. Only then could she begin to fashion the frock.

As was her custom, Rhoda enjoyed singing her

hymn while she worked. She had a lovely voice that encouraged anyone within earshot to join in. She was pleased to look over at Sarah who was at least mouthing the words.

Blest be the tie that binds
Our hearts in Christian love!
The fellowship of kindred minds
Is like to that above.

Rhoda started to sway but caught herself. If a neighbor had noticed her by chance doing anything that resembled dancing or moving to the music, she would be accused of committing a heinous crime. Ever present in her mind was the knowledge that her fellow townsfolk were anxious to link nefarious conduct to her anyway they could. They were of the mind that her very existence threatened their community. *No matter that I have yet to turn a cart loaded over with hay merely by my glance or cause a cow to produce a still-born heifer.*

A fortnight ago Mr. Philbrook accused her of taking the form of a sheep and reading his thoughts. She could laugh at such nonsense if these ridiculous accusations were not accompanied with such vehemence and ugly expressions. Fortunately, there was little proof the townspeople could muster and had to be satisfied with merely spreading the gossip.

Amazingly, the fact that the Weare inhabitants perceived Rhoda as a witch did not interfere with their business. She maintained a low profile while her husband worked in their tavern. The magnetic pull of spiritous liquors was stronger than their superstitions. On occasion, she overheard a customer who, falling under the influence of the strong ale or rum, bandied about a joke directed at her, but William ignored them. They had agreed it was better to swallow the urge to punch someone in the nose than to lose a paying customer. William would clench his fists, but keep them at his side.

Reuben maintained an eye on his mother. When he perceived she was about ready to ladle out their meal, he hovered nearby to line up directly behind his father, whose position in the family guaranteed that he first to be served. The Feeble Four would not dare push or shove him with his father near, and he was assured of getting a trifle more beans than if he were at the end of the line.

He carried his steaming beans to the sitting room where he managed to secure the solitary chair near the hearth. A dining room with a table and chairs for every family member was a luxury the Favors had only heard about. Many times they consumed theirs meals standing or crowded on the edge of the pull-down bed.

Reuben started to put the bowl to his lips. His brothers entered, giggling and elbowing each other.

"Leave me be, John!"

"Aw, Moses, you did not spill any. If you had, Reuben here could lick 'em up for you!"

Reuben rolled his eyes and escaped outside to eat in peace. The moon, gray and unremarkable, was already in the evening sky. Thin clouds trailed over the dull light. He sniffed in the musty air and plodded toward the barn. The trees were dark giants waving and peering down on him—soon to bear witness to his unfortunate blunder. He sat down with his legs stretched out in front and his back pushed against the rough exterior of the barn boards.

First, he picked up the few pieces of pork fat. After devouring them and sucking the greasy remains off his fingers, he raised the bowl to his mouth and sucked in some beans. Then he used his index finger to push the remaining beans to the rim; he slurped them one by one and licked the wooden bowl.

His belly asked for more; however, he closed his eyes and attempted to concentrate on the music of the evening. A soft wind pushed against the branches above him. A few leaves rustled as they filtered through the long arms and skinny fingers of a stately maple. Reuben exhaled a deep sigh that made his lips flutter. He surveyed the area for something to do and settled on twirling the stem of a leaf that had floated within reach. Slowly, an idea began to form in his young brain.

Reuben scurried around, bent over like an old man, gathering dried grass, last year's brittle leaves, and twigs. He mounded them into a pyramid. He retrieved the flint from his pocket and sat down against the barn with his legs in a V and the pyramid of debris between them. Reuben was well aware of the dangers of fire. He simply felt that he could manipulate it as easily as he manipulated everything in his life.

He struck his knife against the flint three times with no success. The fourth attempt produced a spark that hopped onto the dry grass and leaves as if drawn by a magnetic force. Reuben blew gently and smoke swirled and caressed his face. A small flame began to wiggle. He shielded it with cupped hands, blew on it, and fed it with twigs, one by one. Firelight illuminated his breeches. What he failed to recognize was an alliance developing between the evening breeze and the flames.

The flame nibbled at the dry leaves and grass near his crotch and included them in its choreography. Reuben sprang to his feet, jumped to the side, and stared in horror as the flames quickly grew taller and ate a wider swath. In seconds it would lick the barn. Reuben continued to stare in terror, transfixed as if his feet were embedded in the earth and his body was made of stone. He had not expected it to travel.

Fire was a capricious friend, and its betrayal was holding Reuben under its spell.

A piercing scream woke him from his trance. His mother had come outside to look for him and saw the unmistakable flickering illumination from around the corner of the barn. Hearing her scream "FIRE!" three times in rapid succession produced other family members who poured out of the house as if chased by a swarm of bees. Mr. Favor was shouting orders in between curses. Mistress Favor was crying. Reuben's brothers snatched up buckets as they dashed to the cistern. In one swift motion, they dunked the buckets and scooped up the water. Bucket after bucket sloshed up the line of the brigade. The one throwing the water made a mad dash to the end of the line where the bucket was frantically loaded again.

During this period of chaos, Reuben, with his heart attempting to break out of his chest, had stumbled off to the side. The dancing flames commanded everyone's attention, and he found himself alone—alone to form his story. Reuben collapsed onto a log. His mind skirted in five different directions trying to develop a plausible reason to exonerate himself for the fire that was starting to consume their barn. The smoke wafted in his direction, stung his eyes, and burned his nostrils. He didn't dare interrupt his concentration by moving away; instead he bowed his head, supported it in the palm of his left hand, and cupped his forehead. His fingers drummed across his matted hair.

Reuben's eyes moved to his right hand. His fingers were curled into a tight fist. He released his fingers one by one. The flint. It had left an imprint in his palm. He rubbed the hard stone between his thumb and two fingers as if to help conjure up a good story or excuse. Somehow, he needed to convince them he was not to blame, but the flint would not protect his story.

The ground had become a soggy mess of wet leaves, mud, and puddles. Smoke curled in taunting tendrils from the side of the barn, soon to explode in flames. The smell permeated the air and seeped into everyone's clothing. He knew it would linger in the fabric long after, to remind his brothers of his transgression. Forever in the future, if ever another verbal retort failed to come to mind, they could always resort to recalling his sin—unless he came up with a convincing story. Within minutes, the family had exhausted the water in the cistern and could only stand helplessly by, staring at the flames licking and eating up their barn. The barn that held the freshly cut hay, planks of pine to build an addition to the house, and stalls for the horses they were hoping to buy.

His father was bent at the waist and overwhelmed with a coughing fit. His mother slapped his back and tried to offer some comfort. Reuben positioned himself several paces behind and fashioned a faraway blank stare.

Betsey was the first to address Reuben. "We lost our barn with no thanks to you, Reuben!" Her voice rose to a shrill scream. The other siblings echoed her recriminations.

Mr. Favor threw his bucket down with such fury it broke into several pieces. He bellowed, "I have never failed to remind all of ye children that fire is *not* to be played with—under *any* circumstances!"

He stormed toward Reuben with his hand raised. If Reuben had not been concentrating on fixing his stare on a distant point beyond the hayfield, his father's furious expression would have unsettled him enough to wet his breeches. Maintaining the blank stare as if in a trance and keeping his body rigid, he slowly lifted his arm and pointed in the direction of his regard. He willed his hand to be steady. He spouted gibberish in the deepest voice he could muster. That was enough to puzzle his father and halt his advancing steps. Confused, Mr. Favor's eyes followed the direction of Reuben's arm. Not seeing anything, he grabbed Reuben and was about to throttle him when Reuben growled in a strange voice.

"The witch! The witch!"

Despite tightening his grip on Reuben, Mr. Favor's body went still. His sisters screamed, and his brothers either scanned the hayfield or stared at Reuben, slack-jawed.

"What did you say, Reuben?!"

Mistress Favor had squeezed between her son and husband and was clutching Reuben's shoulders, stooping to peer into his eyes. She shook him and repeated her question.

As if awakened from a deep sleep, Reuben stammered, "The witch, Mmm-mistress Dustin was hhh-ere."

He widened his worried eyes and burned his gaze into his mother's.

"She saw me and asked for a bit of my beans, but I was done and told her likewise. She grew sorrily vexed!" He started to babble, "Steam came out from her presence! I was truly frightened! I feared she was about to harm me; she flung her arm up at the barn where I was sitting and flames started at the base! I had to jump away not to get burned! Then she flew across the hayfield!"

Mistress Favor clutched Reuben and pushed his head into her ample bosom. While her arms wrapped him with maternal concern, she stared at her husband. She mouthed the words, "What are we going to do?"

"Fetch the lad more to drink!" Reuben's father called to his wife. "We need enough urine to get a good boil roilin'!"

Mr. Favor stood over Reuben and frowned at the scant yellow pee in the pot. Joseph handed his mother the dripping pitcher of cider. She filled Reuben's mug for the third time. Reuben developed a tremor, not so much from the fright of the experience or being forced to pee in front of his family, but from the cold cider Joseph's shaky hand had spilled down his back. He decided to use the tremor to his advantage.

Mistress Favor pushed the embers around in the fireplace and added another log. Orange flames flared up and around the dry wood.

"Are you sure 'twill work, Husband?"

"Mr. Bailey told me this morning to boil Reuben's urine whilst keepin' a death-like silence. 'Twill surely kill the witch."

"My insides are still scrambled from yesterday eve. I fear that I may be issuin' blood soon."

"Stop your talkin' and drink the cider. If that fails,

we'll give you some ale."

Mr. Favor pushed his chin down into his soiled stock to study Reuben. Reuben suspected his father cared few beans about his welfare but instead feared Mistress Dustin would return to do more harm to their homestead. Keeping his gaze focused on Reuben he paced back and forth as if willing him to urinate.

Within the hour Reuben had filled enough of the pot to start the boiling. Mrs. Favor placed the iron pot on the swinging arm and positioned it directly over the flames.

"Nary a word for this to function and take Mistress Dustin to task!" Mr. Favor glared at all the children one by one.

Betsey scooped up Rebecca and left the kitchen to wait in the sitting room. Everyone else squeezed together, staring at the pot as if expecting Mistress Dustin's likeness to float out. Slowly, steam rose and the strong stench of urine rose to their nostrils. John pinched his nose. Joseph and Moses made faces at each other. The fetid smell became stronger as the urine raged in the pot. John backed away. In doing so, he stepped on twelve-year old Cutting's toes, and Cutting emitted a high-pitched shriek.

"You could win a contest squealin' louder than a pig stuffed in a flour sack!" John wailed back. Thinking he was being funny, he looked around to get mutual appreciation of his comment—only to see horrified looks.

"John! Your attention span does not outlast that of

a pine beetle's! The spell is broken!" Mr. Favor yelled as he pushed John out of his way and stormed out of the house, his wife trailing behind.

"Where are you goin', Husband?"

"I expect to have words with Mistress Dustin!"

He disappeared into a shed and emerged with a broad axe over his shoulder. His wife's hand flew to her mouth as she sucked in a mouthful of air. She thought she tasted the remains of their barn. She turned her worried glance toward the house and then back again. Her hand fluttered around her mouth and was fixing to call his name, but then she changed her mind; he was headstrong, nothing she could say would stop him. She watched the resolute figure march at a fast clip down the dirt road and disappear, beginning his long walk from Barnard Hill to Dustin's Tavern. *If this act of violence means our dear Reuben and our farm will be spared, I shall have to accept and pardon it.* She turned on her heel and went back inside.

"That's it, hold her tight, Son. She won't be likin' this."

William Dustin's arm disappeared up the cow's back end as Peter constrained her head, averting his eyes to avoid her frantic, wild look. William's hand, small for a man's, groped inside for the calf's head. A steamy, pungent odor overwhelmed the sweet scent of this year's hay, now mixed with blood, manure, and amniotic fluid. The hooves protruded with each strain and then retracted. There hadn't been progress for over an hour.

"Something is seriously wrong. She should have delivered that calf already."

William looked up at his wife. Rhoda's head was cocked to the side; her forehead knitted in empathy for the creature. She gripped her sides.

"There, there girl. 'Twill be over soon," she clucked in a whisper, "one way or t'other."

"It appears its head has flipped back. Her contractions are endeavorin' to push the blockage out, to no avail." The cow's protests were getting weaker, but he still had to raise his voice to be heard above the agonizing sounds.

"I cannot grasp the neck," he said through gritted teeth as he strained in desperation. The cow expressed her suffering in the most pitiful way, making Rhoda clutch her belly in sympathy.

"We are goin' to lose 'em both, are we not, Husband?"

Her voice sounded defeated. William was not ready to lose the cow for which he had invested so much. She had cost him more than any other cow but had produced more milk than any other. She was not a first calf heifer, having thrown two healthy calves previously. This was not supposed to happen.

"Your hand might be better. Give it a try, Wife."

Rhoda worked her way around William in the cramped stall and positioned herself behind the cow's rump. Sighing, she forced herself to slide her hand up the cramped cavity next to the calf's neck. Her fingers tried to wrap around the hot sogginess and find the point at which the neck was folded back, but she didn't have enough space; the neck was too thick. Disheartened, she pulled her hand out and met her husband's concerned gaze. He stood with his feet apart to maintain balance; he had been up since dawn ministering to the cow and clearly was bearing the brunt of it. He wiped the sweat or tears, she could not determine which, with the inside of his crooked arm. Suddenly, something caught her attention.

Rhoda looked beyond William's shoulder. Either he did not hear her gasp or assumed it was directed at the poor beast. Standing behind William, in the doorway of the barn, loomed five angry-looking men. They were of differing statures and ages, but each wore an expression of outrage. One gripped an ominous broad axe diagonally across his chest. Rhoda Dustin blinked the tears from her eyes and recognized Mr. Favor. Rhoda's fearful face caused William to pivot. For a moment, the two factions only stared at each other. The visitors glowered at the Dustins' bloody arms and the Dustins waited, fearing what they would do next. Peter rose and stood next to his mother.

"We are here to warn, you. Leave my son be!" Mr. Favor's wrath spilled out. He shook the axe and shouted, "Stop botherin' my boy, Reuben! Your interference cost us our barn!"

The three Dustins dared not move but remained perplexed.

"Mistress Dustin! We will not tolerate such crimes as you have recently committed. You have done your last and final!" He held the helve of the axe by two hands and waved it at them. The bellowing of the dying cow cut through the air.

Rhoda dared to cry out, "Truly sir, I do not know of what you speak! We have been here all day trying to save our cow and calf. If you expect that I have powers to bother, you should also expect that I have powers to heal! If that be so, how is it that I am unable to bring the young life out of our precious cow and save her life as well? Surely you must understand that their loss is a grave hardship for us, and if I could, I most assuredly would spend my time savin' them and not do whatever it is you think I did to your boy."

As if on cue, the wretched animal gave her last mournful bellow, perhaps aiding Rhoda to convince the enraged father to take pause.

Mr. Favor dropped the heavy axe to his side. He turned both ways to look at his friends, appearing to read their expressions. Rhoda saw her words had given them reason to think—everyone knew a cow was a valuable commodity. Indeed, if she had the strength they attributed to her, why was she not able to use her ways to save the pitiful beast?

Reuben's father remained angry; the snarl was reluctant to diminish, but the sharp edges of his anger smoothed a fraction.

"I'll not have you tormentin' Reuben," he snapped—or—I shall *kill* you!"

His threat may have been an after-thought, Rhoda noted, but the desperation in his voice was serious. She had an inkling his fury would return if she dared to deny any more interaction, thus giving him license to follow through on his promise.

"Mr. Favor," she began solemnly, trying to overcome her fear, "indeed, if I had anything to do with your Reuben, I shall stop it."

He repeated his outrage several times. His friends grunted or nodded. The Dustins remained silent as each repeated threat and grunt lost a piece of the original venom. Mr. Favor stood as if at a loss of what to do next. Neither Rhoda nor William offered an additional defense. With one last snarl and a humph that sounded more like a wild animal's growl, Mr. Favor stormed away, his posse jogging to keep up with him.

After Mr. Favor had been gone a scant ten minutes from his family, everyone in the house was attempting to go about their business while maintaining a wary eye on Reuben. Reuben surmised that a few ticks and shudders on occasion wouldn't hurt in supporting his accusations against Mistress Dustin. He performed them with expertise when he knew all eyes were on him, and secretly he enjoyed making his mother wince. Reuben turned the flint over in his pocket. Somehow, he needed to return it to its rightful place before his mother noticed it missing. He waited until he thought no one was watching him and drew it out of his pocket.

John stood off to the side, frowning. Reuben didn't dare look directly at him but was certain that John was troubled by something—and it wasn't sympathy. John stepped closer. Cutting followed him. Reuben quickly put his hand behind his back.

"What are you hidin', Brother?" John cocked his head around to look behind Reuben. Reuben twisted away from him. John nodded to Cutting, who walked behind Reuben. Reuben whipped his tight fist in front of him and pressed it against his chest.

"You got something clutched in your hand. What could it be? John taunted.

"What could it be?" repeated Cutting in the same tone, now standing next to John.

"'Tis only that I have palpitations and 'tis hard to breathe." Reuben pounded his closed fist against his chest. He hoped his brothers didn't detect the tremor in his voice.

Reuben retreated backwards as his two brothers got closer and closer. Moses and Joseph joined them; John's accusatory tone had alerted them to something suspicious transpiring. The Feeble Four were so close Reuben could smell and feel their rancid breaths against his face. He was trapped with his back plastered to the bed attached to the wall.

Two events happened simultaneously: Mistress Favor, having heard a disturbance with Reuben's frightened voice, spilled into the room just as John crashed the bed down on Reuben. Reuben opened his fist to protect the fall.

"Has not the poor boy been tormented enough?" she yelled.

She was about to grab the scruff of the closest boy's neck when something slid out from Reuben's hand, skimmed across the wood floor, and stopped at her feet. She gave it a startled look with a jerk of her head, put her hands on her hips, and then stooped to retrieve it. The flint. Reuben's back was turned. Tears of indignation from the attack and pain welled in Reuben's eyes. Momentarily, he forgot about the flint and slammed the bed back into position. He twisted around to see his mother staring at the flint in her hand.

Reuben froze. He watched his mother's confused expression dissolve into disappointment, then go to anger.

He winced, clutched at his shoulder, and emitted a pitiful whine. Then he staggered. He peered at her to see if it produced the customary sympathy and support; however, her expression remained unchanged.

The Feeble Four were like heroic statues: They stood still with hands on their hips and chests puffed out. Reuben narrowed his eyes and clenched his teeth at the triumphant look on John's face. Their mother's shoulders slowly slumped.

Reuben's mouth hung open. His eyebrows arched into his forehead, widening his eyes enough for the whites to encircle the clear, blue irises. A wash of emotions swept across him—first, vexation directed at his brothers for slamming the bed on top of him, then frustration that his standard repertoire of compassion-inducing ploys for the benefit of his mother was not working, and finally, fear with the realization that they were about to accuse him of starting the fire. His head whipped around to look at each person.

"She humbugged me," his voice cracked as he babbled, "from the other day she passed me on the road! She changed my person. The wink! The wink she gave me turned me into a terrible, troublesome boy! I may look the same, but I am *not!*" His imploring tone and frantic look had little effect. Tears ran down his chubby cheeks.

"Reuben started the fire!" John yelled. "Why else would he be hidin' the flint?"

"Indeed! Why does he even *need* a flint?" added Moses.

The toddler wobbled over to his mother. In one fell swoop, Mistress Favor picked him up, jutted her hip out, and perched the child on top. She stormed out of the room into the kitchen, bouncing the delighted child with each step. His sisters appeared out of nowhere to get an explanation regarding the ruckus. The four boys were either bent at their waists moaning and clutching their sides to mock Reuben or slapping their thighs in laughter. Reuben ran after his mother.

"Dear Mother, I . . ." He stopped. Never before had he witnessed her anger directed solely at him. Her stare crept from outrage to disappointment. He noted a sadness in her expression that he had never seen before.

For the first time, Reuben felt something strange in the pit of his stomach. He had the unfamiliar urge to wrap his arms around his mother and hold her tight.

She put the toddler down, gripped Reuben's shoulders, and shook him. "You took the flint, which all here knows full-well, is *not* allowed without askin', and you burned the barn down." She paused. "Mistress Dustin had nothin' to do with the fire. Did she?" She strengthened her grip and shook his shoulders harder. Reuben couldn't answer; he was wailing and hiccuping.

"*Did* she?" his mother yelled.

Reuben wiped his runny nose on his sleeve and stopped snuffling long enough to repeat one last time in desperation in a faint, pathetic voice, "She humbugged me." At the same time, he mustered his secret weapon that had never failed him before: his well-honed, doe-eyed, and deep stare into his mother's eyes.

"It seems to me that if one were changed by humbuggery, one would nary know it," she started in a slow and steady voice that built up speed. "You have not been humbugged; I fear it has been *me* that has been humbugged, and *you* have been doin' it!"

"Did not we try to tell ye this all along, Mother?" John protested, his pitch rising as he tried to be heard above Reuben's sobbing. "You have always held Reuben blameless, and we have suffered fer it!"

The other brothers' heads bobbed and nodded as if they were attached to springs. The rest of his siblings held their peace and simply stared wide-eyed at

Reuben, who was dissolving into a convulsive, blubbering mess on the floor.

It was dusk when Mr. Favor arrived home. The men had peeled off one by one and returned to their wives to discuss the situation with Reuben and the witch. Few words had been exchanged on the journey; the fires that raged in their bellies on the trip to the Dustins, stoked by Mr. Favor, were dying embers on the way home. But they still burned.

Reuben's father was not wholly convinced that Mistress Dustin did not interfere with his son; however, the long walk home helped him calm down. Still, he clung to his anger as if it comforted him: It was a lot easier to believe the witch burned his barn than his son. He put the axe in the shed and stumbled into the house. The children were asleep. Reuben had exhausted himself with all his wailing. The last vestige of his energy had been depleted by one final exaggerated, dramatic fling on the floor that was clearly wasted. Finally, in a hoarse whisper, Reuben had admitted he set the barn afire. Mistress Favor met her husband in the doorway. If he wasn't looking down he would have noticed her puffy eyes and knitted brows.

He dropped heavily into the chair by the fire while she informed him of the flint and Reuben's confession. He stared at the floor with his elbows resting on his knees and ran his hand through his graying hair. The pieces to the puzzle were starting to come together, but both were hesitant to admit that Reuben might have been lying, all the while using Mistress Dustin's wink to escape his chores and to receive special treatment.

"You always coddled that boy, Wife. Set him free from your skirts and let him grow to be a man of substance!"

With that, Mr. Favor rose and yanked the bed down. Reuben woke. He dared not move in his bedroll—*best to wait to get my thrashing in the morrow.*

Superstitions etched in the consciousness of a people are hard to smooth out. The outcome like the one with Reuben and the maligned Mistress Dustin caused the good colonists of Weare to begin opening their minds like a tightly wrapped rosebud slowly releasing its petals. Perhaps Rhoda Dustin had no power to interfere with the health and welfare of man and beast. The accusations and finger-pointing did not come to an abrupt halt but became fewer and further between. After much time had passed and new settlers arrived, the belief in witches gradually disappeared all together.

For all the prejudice Rhoda Dustin experienced in her lifetime, *The History of Weare* recorded, "All this was a dreadful scandal on Mistress Dustin, who was a very nice woman."

TIMOTHY CORLISS:
AN INDIAN
HOSTAGE

January 1810

$\mathcal{T}$he old man's time on this earth was nearing the end. Perhaps he had already left it . . . in his mind, anyway. His gnarled, quivering hands clenched the bed sheets while disturbing memories swirled in his head. His sightless eyes unmasked the horror playing in his mind.

"He seems troubled, Doctor. I thought you said he was resting comfortably."

A woman in her mid-thirties sat next to his bedside and tried to caress the old man's cheek with the back of her hand. He recoiled as if being scalded. The tearful woman, who knew this shell of a man as her once robust father, winced and snapped her hand back in response. She tried to calm him with the same soothing tone he had used with her many years ago.

Suddenly, his eyes grew wider. A female figure with a grotesque grimace had materialized, taunting him and waving a torch in his direction. He tensed and rose a few inches, his frail state not allowing him to sit up. His hand fluttered in the air, the arthritic index finger shaking but unmistakably pointing at something in the far corner of the room. He gaped at a specter the others in the room could not see. His lips attempted to form a word but instead a whine escaped, like that of an animal in great pain. His energy spent, the woman managed to ease him gently back onto the goose down pillow that cradled his head.

"I believe his mind has wrapped around those awful months in captivity, Doctor, and is reluctant to release him from the torment. It was so long ago, would that he could relive more pleasant times. He never talked about the trials of his kidnapping, as much as we children begged. He simply said that it was all in the past, and he chose not to dredge it up. He suffered with the Indians for a year until my grandfather was able to gather the ransom and release him."

"It appears the nightmare never left him, Madam. Surely, the laudanum will help. Soon the torment of the ordeal will fade away."

Freedom Lost

October 1746

The twenty-year-old trapper slogged along the snowy edge of the Peacock Brook, a branch of the Piscataquog, to survey the extent of the beaver activity. The beaver had felled most of the willows and poplars within an acre. Well-established canals, a little more than a foot deep and two feet wide, stretched from the wooded area to the river bank, allowing the beaver to move logs to their dam or lodge with ease. Timothy Corliss surveyed the thinned woods and the amount of construction. *They may have exhausted their food source. Perhaps they have already left, but if I do not set this trap, I shall never know for sure.*

The lodge was impressive. The dome-shaped structure rose out of the water as if on an island. The rodents had made a sturdy home with logs, scores of branches, mud, and rocks skillfully plastered together. Pole tips leaned in the same direction as the water flowed. Once, out of curiosity, Timothy and his brother had dismantled part of an abandoned lodge. They discovered a platform about six inches above the water level that could keep the kits warm and dry in the winter. Unfortunately for the diligent creatures, Timothy's admiration for their industriousness was exceeded only by his need to barter their pelts.

Timothy had his eye on a 62-caliber flintlock rifle with a curly maple stock and a forty-two-inch barrel. A squirrelly friend of his father's had bought it in Haverhill and told Timothy he would agree to a trade of twelve beaver pelts. Not sure the man could be trusted, Timothy was nevertheless bound and determined to try to make the trade. He had four more to trap before the man was due to go back to Haverhill, one week hence. If he could trap one beaver a day, he might make the quota and have enough time to find the man. Indeed, a rifle would ensure more accurate shooting than his musket.

At present, the musket he had was not very efficient. One missed shot, which was all too common, not only yielded dense smoke, but a sound loud enough to scare all the game away, as well as awaken the dead. Afterward, it was useless to get out another ball and powder for deployment. A musket was simply not suited for hunting. For the time being, he would have to be satisfied with trapping.

He set his sack down and rubbed his hands together to warm his fingers. He inhaled the musty smell carried on the sudden blast of autumn wind. It tore off many of the remaining tenacious, scarlet and yellow leaves and sent them spiraling into the river and floating away. He pulled out the heavy chain and steel trap he had scented with beaver oil. Timothy wrinkled his nose at the pungent smell cutting through the cool air. *I should be used to it by now.* He unsheathed the hatchet hanging from his sash and went about searching for saplings.

His eagerness to set the trap overleaped caution and he forgot to look where he was stepping. His foot snapped a dead branch leaning across a small rock. He froze, held his breath, and listened. He had no desire to be the hunted one. He had heard rumors of the Indians being on the warpath and feared they were thick in the woods. It was possible to encounter an Indian or two hoping to trade a white man to the French in Canada. *I wonder what price I could bring . . .*

Growing up in Haverhill, Massachusetts Bay Colony, Timothy often went to bed listening to his parents discussing the horrific stories of Indian raids and kidnappings. Three decades before his birth in 1726, several bloody Indian raids had claimed the lives of dozens of men, women, and children. Timothy knew all about the details of Hannah Dustin's miraculous escape with his kin Mary Corliss Neff. They returned home with scalps from the same Indians that had killed three of Hannah's children, but not before the Indians had forced them on a brutal, late winter trek, for weeks at a time, toward Canada. Timothy was well-versed in the tactics the survivors used to avoid the sharp end of a tomahawk in their skull. Parents repeated the sorrowful lessons learned, hoping they would never be needed. Soon, Timothy would be grateful for the instruction.

If Indians were near, they could easily pick up on the snapping sound of a branch, even one muffled by dead leaves. After a few minutes, fixed to the spot by his own circumspection, he continued, but he slowed his movements and watched where he stepped.

Working silently, he selected two small but sturdy branches for his trap. Using his hatchet, he peeled away the thin skin of the bark. He tucked the sticks under his arm and headed back to the river's edge where he had left his trapping tools. He dug into his sack once more to retrieve a bottle of castor oil and dipped one of the naked sticks to scent it with the bait.

During the unseasonably cold night, a thin layer of ice had formed at the edge of the stream. He jabbed the stick into the delicate icy skim, and then like a blind man testing his footing, he slid one boot into the frigid water; he waited patiently while his foot settled on a flat surface. He slid his other foot in, took a deep breath, and exhaled a long, slow stream of mist. Timothy teetered a bit until he got his balance, firmly planting the second foot. He did not have a change of clothes in the event he tumbled into the brook, the level of which had recently grown higher with the autumn rain and run-offs from the many springs. Getting his breeches a little wet was one thing, but a full-body plunge would be inconvenient, to be sure.

Timothy placed the trap three inches below the surface of the water and jammed the prepared stick into its jaws. With the second stick he staked the chain in the deeper part of the river.

If there were beaver in the lodge, they would appear soon. With their acute sense of smell and instinctive curiosity, beaver would be attracted to the bait. Timothy started to gather his belongings near the stream's edge, but turned to marvel one moment longer at their lodge. *Some lads in Haverhill could benefit by learning the work habits of these little animals.* A smile stretched across his ruddy face and his clear blue eyes glinted thinking of his two younger brothers. His smile quickly dissipated.

A low-flying eagle gliding above caught Timothy's eye. But what he noticed in the distance beyond the graceful flight gave him pause: smoke rising into the sky—*could be an Indian campfire*. He wasted no time reacting to the potential danger. Snatching up the rest of his possessions, he ran back into the water. He jogged as best he could in the bed of the stream to conceal his tracks. His boots slid on the mossy rocks and he had to balance his pack not to fall or drop it into the water. He looked over his shoulder and judged the smoke to be far enough away that the Indians would not hear his splashing.

Timothy arrived at his camp with ice clinging to

the wisps of his mustache. He and his father had chosen this spot a few years earlier because of an overhanging granite ledge. They had piled large stones to make walls on the north and west ends. He pulled out his moose-hide mittens and got to work replenishing the rafters with spruce and covering them with bark for a decent ceiling. He tossed in moss, dry leaves, green spruce and hemlock boughs to fashion a comfortable bed. With hands on his hips, he inhaled the sweet smell of the evergreens. *The late October sun is not going to shed light forever; I need to get a fire going soon.*

He sat down on a log and dug into his pack for a flint. His feet were cold and itchy inside his wet boots. He stood and ran in place to warm them up then scurried around to scoop up kindling to make a fire. The fire might alert Indians to his location, but they rarely attacked at night; they preferred to surprise their target in a predawn slumber. He would have to make a hasty escape before the sun peered over the tree line.

Two strips of salted beef jerky, one small hunk of dried meat encased in bear fat, and river water was not much but enough to appease his growling stomach. More or less satisfied, he ducked into his makeshift abode. He wiggled his long, thin frame into a comfortable cavity, expelled a long breath, and fell asleep.

The next morning, Timothy left the camp as soon as he was able to see his mittened hand before his face. He was anxious to get the blood flowing. It had been a very long and cold night. He hiked at a fast pace back to check on his trap but stopped every once in a while, alert to the sounds around him. Birds sang their morning songs and swooped down to skim the water; the pines swayed to their cheerful music.

No sooner had he begun to shrug off the predawn cold than he had to wade once again into the cold water. He felt around the stake, pulled up the chain, and was rewarded with a medium-sized female beaver, about twenty-four inches from nose to base of tail. *Three more to go, and the rifle is mine!*

He stopped at the edge of the water and imagined the good hunting he and his father would enjoy after getting the rifle. Any month with an R in it meant good thick fur on the animals. *We have a pile of good hunting yet to do. With all the animal tracks I have seen on this trip alone, I contend these parts will yield many quality pelts and plenty of meat as well.*

The wind picked up; branches rubbed and swayed to create the creaking sounds of forest music. Water splashed over the exposed rocks. The thin layer of ice cracked up and down the bank. The sounds of nature formed an alliance with the stealthy Indian slowly creeping toward Timothy.

In one rapid motion, the Abenaki wrapped his arms firmly around the trapper's arms and gripped him as tight as a vice. Timothy reacted with a twist, but the Indian locked his hands and clenched him against his chest. Timothy felt the warmth of the measured breathing in his ear and smelled the unpleasant bear grease in the long black hair. His heart thumped wildly;

his tongue parched as dry as cotton. *Relax, relax, relax . . .*

The elders' voices rang in his head, "Indians respect courage but punish resistance. Show strength through compliance." Remaining calm after an initial attack was the common thread among survivors. Timothy swallowed hard to keep the meager contents of his stomach down. *I cannot let them see my fear. Stay calm, stay calm.*

He instructed his tensed muscles to relax and concentrated on easing his breathing. His exhalations were visible in the chilly air. Gradually, the Indian released his grip but grabbed Timothy's hands and tied them behind his back with a leather thong. The Indian was not alone; two others were currently engaged in pilfering his possessions: One was rifling through his pack, the other was bent over, deftly eviscerating the beaver. All three wore breechcloths but otherwise were naked. They were indeed products of the wilderness, their russet bodies sculpted from chasing after game.

If he was going to lose his scalp, it would have happened by now. Timothy tried to let that thought comfort him. The Indian pointed to the ground and Timothy sunk down next to a tree. The one who had gone through his pack jammed everything back inside and made a comment to Timothy's guard who responded with a nod. The third one, a strong, fierce-looking warrior had a ragged, pink scar that ran from his right earlobe and disappeared in a crease next to his mouth; he held the beaver's steaming entrails up and let the blood course down his arm. With a lopsided smirk, he licked the sticky, scarlet rivulet with one long swipe of his tongue and then tossed the mass off to one side. He showed no sign of wanting to wash the rest of the blood off his hands. The second coppery-faced Indian skinned the beaver, tied meat and pelt in balls, and added them to the pack along with the coveted tail, destined for their sachem.

The scarred Indian pumped his hand, palm up, and Timothy stood up. His legs felt weak, he started to shiver all over, and, with his hands tied behind his back, he almost lost his balance. *Steady, steady.* He spread his weight evenly over his stance and bent his knees to gain control over his muscles.

The two Indians called the one with a scar Bezo and shouted to him. Timothy felt a hand on his back. A strong push. *Is it to help me?* Bezo shoved Timothy in line behind the two others. Bezo barked a command, and Timothy began to jog in line with the Indians.

After jogging half an hour from the abduction site, and most likely feeling secure that no colonists were on their trail, the natives started to don the warmer clothing they had stashed. Even in winter, the Indians attacked wearing nothing more than breechcloths of doeskin suspended from their belts; Timothy thought them impervious to the cold air. Now each had a mantle of hide fastened over one shoulder to allow full motion of the opposite arm that was covered in a different skin. The fur was worn next to their bodies and the hide tucked into belts. On their legs they wore tubes of deerskin suspended from the belt with lateral thongs sewn with rawhide strips through perforated holes on the outside; decorated gators held the leggings tight against the lower leg. Beaver pelt moccasins adorned their feet. Bezo sported a deer tail that wagged from his mantle with each step.

One of the Indians started a fire; it crackled, and Timothy shuddered. A series of embers shot up and twirled in the air, lost their energy, and disappeared. The Indian had wrapped the rawhide tight around his hands and feet, but he couldn't fetter the young man's mind. The captive retraced his actions of six hours ago, not for the first time, to relive where he went amiss and to curse his carelessness. He had always been cautious. He was attuned to nature and its sounds, but the surreptitious Indian succeeded in taking him by surprise. Timothy Corliss had let his guard down. *All I was thinkin' about was gettin' the blasted rifle by trapping a few more beaver. In one respect, I am relieved father cannot see me in this present humiliatin' and debilitative state.* He did not want to even entertain his mother's reaction.

Timothy leaned against the rough bark of the huge white pine and stared at the flickering flames. He hoped his captors intended to feed him tonight. Bezo and another native had disappeared. The remaining man searched the area for more dry wood. Timothy heard him snapping and hacking branches into shorter lengths. He took the opportunity to tug at the strips of rawhide around his hands. The Indian had used a unique method to tie the constraints; the more

Timothy pulled, the tighter they became. He inhaled a deep breath and puffed it back out through his lips like a horse, bowing his head in resignation. *I would not get very far even if I could break loose.*

Voices carried through the air. The strange sounds meant nothing to the young man, but the tone was clear. One of the Indians was giving orders. Timothy craned his head around to see the two Indians, Bezo and the short, barrel-chested one he called Atian, followed by a sorry cluster of three white people and three more Indians herding them toward the makeshift camp. *Misery loves company.* The Indian tending to the fire rose and studied the frightened people as if he was mentally determining their worth.

The white newcomers stopped at the edge of the clearing. The woman's cap was askew and strands of curly locks had escaped from the unsecured side. One strand covered her left eye, but she made no effort to brush it away. Her trembling hands gripped a fistful of the wool shawl that stretched over her shoulders. Crimson streaks ran the length of her homespun skirt, but she did not appear to be wounded. A tall, thin man wearing a wool hat, blue frock coat, and torn wool stockings stood at her side. His arm circled her waist and he pulled her close to whisper something in her ear. Whatever he said fell on deaf ears: Her blank expression did not change. The third person, a man, was partially hidden behind the couple, but Timothy could see a round face with red cheeks that bore the stress of their ordeal.

When the three new Indians joined the others, five began to yip, dance, and sing. They were carrying on as if in a frenzy. The sixth Indian stood guard over the hostages but yipped along with the others. The singing proceeded into fervent yelling. Timothy had heard from the survivors in his community that this was common after a raid or capture. Whether his prior knowledge of their behavior was expected or not, the fervor caused Timothy's insides to twist.

The new captives huddled together, gripping each other as if needing to combine their strength to remain upright. The two men watched the Indians' spectacle with loose mouths and white-rimmed eyes. The woman's face showed no emotion; she was staring through them to a distant sight, or perhaps memory. When the Indians stopped their brief performance, they turned their attention to the new arrivals.

Bezo pantomimed putting his hands behind his back, and two other Indians proceeded to tie the newcomers in the same fashion as Timothy. Except for the Indians chattering in their mysterious tongue, everyone else remained silent, as if contemplating what they had done to deserve God's wrath.

Bezo pointed to the ground near the base of another tree, next to where Timothy was bound. The native had fine white teeth and not unpleasant features, if viewing his undamaged profile, but his ragged scar on the opposite side accentuated his mean countenance. The three eased themselves down and leaned against a trunk. The white men exchanged frightened looks with each other and then looked despairingly at Timothy. He returned their sorrowful look with a slight smile and lift of his chin, hoping to relay a modicum of encouragement. The woman did not return Timothy's glance. Her eyes were wide, and she continued to stare ahead with a distant, frantic look. It was as if she had witnessed some unspeakable horror. Timothy was certain she had. She shook uncontrollably.

"Steady, mistress. Time to hold onto yer wits," Timothy whispered.

"Not certain we have much of those left," the heavy man replied under his breath. "We had two young ones with us when we . . ." His throat tightened as he failed to get the last of his words out and glanced cautiously at the woman. She did not register hearing his words but remained a victim in her private hell.

"We were nine at the start, but they separated us from our neighbors." He paused and then whispered, "I fear they met the same end as the children in our group."

The fire crackled. A small amount of heat wafted toward the prisoners, and then a cold breeze engulfed them in smoke. The woman started to cough, enough to bring her out of her trance. She began to shake less. She brought her knees up, leaned over, and buried her face into her skirts.

The tall man, on her right side, whispered something that Timothy barely heard. He understood enough to surmise the man, most likely her husband, was trying to persuade her to compose herself for the children's sakes. The couple would need to bury their utter desolation and agony if they ever hoped to see their five-year-old twins again. Whatever it was, she sniffed loudly and sat erect, staring straight ahead, hatred etched into her tear-stained face.

The hostages watched as the six natives roasted and ate the beaver meat that should have been for Timothy. The aroma was now his dinner. *I am not terribly hungry anyway.* He tried to ignore the rumbling in his stomach. His fellow companions didn't indicate any sign of hunger. The Indians took the remaining meat, mashed it with berries they produced, and made it into cakes for portable food. While the Indians were preoccupied working and laughing around the fire, the four took the opportunity to share names and talk.

"Whatever befalls us, it is vital ye do not react. Your survival depends upon it," Timothy began. "They will punish defiance or weakness."

The portly man hunched to his right, Edward McLane, nodded slowly in agreement. "We know only too well what happened in Deerfield. They killed nearly fifty villagers there. More than a hundred were marched to Montreal. The sixty or so that returned had stories . . ." he paused and shot a concerned look at Claire. When she registered nothing, he turned back to Timothy. "Do you suppose that is where we are headed?" he whispered.

"Hard to say at this point, but probably. The fact we remain alive means we are worth something to them . . . as long as we can endure the march."

Timothy saw the sweat dripping from Mr. McLane's temples and noted the roundness of his belly. "You must strive to put one foot in front of the other and be no worse for the wear. We shall most likely be sold to the French in Canada. If we are fortunate, we shall be ransomed." Timothy leaned his head back and looked skyward as he thought about his father not having a shilling to his name, even though they existed well enough by hunting and bartering.

Claire's husband, Henry Clarke, leaned forward to address Timothy. "How in God's name do you expect we shall manage to make it to Canada? We are nearing winter; we have weeks ahead of us on foot, and snow will fall with frigid temperatures."

"I have spent many a fortnight hunting and trapping in the winter. We can manage. It shall not be easy," Timothy flicked his head toward Claire, "but we can do it." Her eyes slowly peered between the stiffened strands of hair. Her steely stare acknowledged his reference, but otherwise, she remained hushed.

Their wardens ignored them until they had finished with the beaver meat. Bezo rose, his eyes burned into Timothy's, and brandishing his two-and-a-half-foot-long tomahawk in the young man's direction, waved it around his head as if to show off, or perhaps to gain some momentum before whacking his head. A thought flew across the young trapper's mind: *It would be a swift death; a second blow would not be necessary.* The frightened captives tensed every muscle. Their shoulders rose and hugged their necks. Timothy squeezed his eyes shut.

Every fiber of his being wanted to react with a terrified scream, but he pressed his lips together to prevent any escape . . . but there was no skull-cracking blow. Timothy peered through narrowed eyes. Bezo was standing over him; his jeering expression was inches from Timothy's perplexed face. The Indian emitted a triumphant laugh. He garbled something to his compatriots, who enjoyed the joke as much as any tavern customer would enjoy a good rum-induced story.

To taunt the captives more, the Indian chopped off a white pine branch hanging above their heads and chuckled as it fell on top of them, needles raining all over them. Timothy and the others shook them off with no comment. Bezo smirked and continued to dance around the makeshift camp. To the captives' relief, he left to join the others slicing off small hemlock and spruce branches for bedding. After completing their chore, the natives sat down. What happened next confirmed Timothy's speculation they were destined to be sold to the French.

Each Indian produced a string of beads. The mood changed as if a curtain had been drawn: The seriousness was in stark contrast to the recent display of childish emotion. If the rawhide constraints had not dug into Timothy's wrists, and if he was not apprehensive about his future, he might have laughed at the dramatic transition. With heads bent, the Indians solemnly mumbled their prayers while fingering their glass beads.

Timothy turned to his fellow captives, "Jesuit

influence. These Indians consider themselves in service to the French."

"The Jesuit priests may have taught the savages the rites of the Catholic Church, but they failed to extract the savage from him," Claire hissed.

"Dear Wife, we cannot fail to remind ourselves, through our own prayers, that our dear Lord has brought us a great challenge, not from displeasure of us, but for his never-ending love. We have been tasked with manifesting our love for Him, despite the circumstances," Henry whispered to remind her that the survivors of the Indian abductions had claimed their faith was responsible for winning their freedom.

"Do you not consider the trial he has delivered unto us excessively severe to demonstrate our devotion?" Tears started in her eyes.

Timothy tried to change the course of the conversation that was steering toward an argument, "We must find solace and some measure of comfort in our religious instruction. We must not give in to these circumstances. We must be strong if we have any desire to return home. I presume there are others who are anxious for your return?" *A heated discussion at present would not be beneficial and would reveal a vulnerability that could be fatal. A focus on the future is the only way to survive.*

The sun was sinking and darkness began to envelope them. Timothy's blanket was nothing more than a cold dampness. A penetrating chill seeped into his bones. His belly groaned again. His wrists burned. *'Twill be a very long night.*

Timothy had always relied on his father's survival teachings in the wilderness and the skills he mastered. *I am determined to prevail. If I can help these poor souls, all the better for it. If God sees fit to abandon or protect me, I will have little say about it anyway. I may as well strive to help myself and pray He will provide me the courage to do so.*

Timothy and the others had intermittent moments of sleep, their harsh accommodations competing with their comfort; however, at predawn he was dreaming of trapping more beaver near the Piscataquog River. He awakened to a searing need to relieve himself. He saw the others squirming, and fortunately, the Indians were sympathetic to their need. Atian cut their bonds and indicated with a flick of his head to walk behind the trees beyond the campfire. He picked up his tomahawk, raised it, and shook it in the air as a warning not to bolt; they did not doubt his threat.

When the four returned, they were witness once again to the mumbling of prayers and the working of rosary beads. Timothy puzzled over the disparity between the natives' acceptance of the teachings of Christ coupled with their barbarous behavior that the survivors of the Haverhill massacre related. The Indians had managed to embrace Christianity as well as adhere to their cultural traditions that were in direct conflict with the former. *Perhaps they learned of the passage in the Bible about "an eye for an eye" which gave them license to continue torturing and murdering innocent people. After all, the white man had not always been gentle with them. One thing was certain, I cannot rely on their Christianity for any comfort or assistance. They are about as mean-spirited and unstable as stallions without a mare.*

The six natives pushed the four white people toward a small path that cut through the trees. Timothy massaged his sore wrists while ducking low-hanging branches. *What can I concentrate on to get my mind off my discomfort and fear? My pleasure in life is hunting and surviving in the wilderness. This circumstance adds a distinct twist to my favorite activity, but I have to imagine that it is no different.* The Indians picked up the pace. The air was cold and each exhale produced a fine mist.

Timothy was not sure how the Clarkes were faring. Timothy was behind Mr. McLane and the others were behind Timothy with two Indians at their backs urging them to go faster. Mr. McLane was slowing down to a lumber and had been sucking in air for the last fifteen minutes. He was Timothy's height but twenty years older and more than thirty pounds heavier; he was not accustomed to jogging in the woods. Timothy needed to space himself back a bit. If he was too close to Edward McLane, he would not see a protruding rock in time or avoid a branch whipping him in the face. But behind him, Atian was getting impatient. A strong push hurled Timothy forward. He tripped, almost lunging against Edward's back, which certainly would have toppled the poor man, but Timothy's nimble side-hop avoided the impact.

Suddenly, a high-pitched yelp from the rear startled Timothy. His instinct was to stop and turn, but the

Indian behind him would most assuredly push him again. *I have to concentrate not to react as I customarily would whilst in the savages' custody.* He allowed himself one quick peek over his shoulder. Claire had fallen. In one way they were in this pickle together and relied on each other; in another, they had to be self-reliant. Helping Claire would only serve to accentuate her weakness and cause trouble for him. Timothy tightened his lips and kept his pace. He honed his hearing with the hope that he would not hear additional disconcerting sounds issuing from behind.

When ten minutes or so had passed without moaning or cries, he decided that Claire was executing well the raised roots and rocks, the long branches, and the occasional brambles that seemed to reach out and grab their clothing. Timothy tried to pick off the burrs from his wool sleeves as he jogged. The thorns and prickers held on tighter and were harder to release. *At least I have buckskin leggings, how must Mistress Clarke cope with her skirts attacked by these annoyances of nature?*

The path threaded through thickets and a few naked maples and birches among the evergreens. The pines dominated in number and height; their straight trunks stretched up to the heavens where they were free to spread out their green arms. Sturdy and solid oaks that proudly stood sentry around their Haverhill home would be dwarfed by the colossal trees. Another time of year, with leaves adorning the branches on the lower-growing trees, Timothy would not have been able to discern the direction where they were jogging, but the flickering light on Mr. McLane's back indicated they were traveling west. *Most likely toward the Contoocook River, and then we shall head north on the Merrimac River. Father said there are villages near the Contoocook River . . . do I dare risk seeking freedom?* For a glorious moment, he allowed himself to dream of good food, a warm bed, and safety. When a branch smacked him in the face, reality reined him in; *even if I manage to liberate myself, they shall do harm to the Clarkes and Mr. McLane for revenge. My life would assuredly meet a dastardly end if they caught me, and indeed, they would catch me.*

The lead Indian came to an abrupt stop. Timothy nearly plowed into Mr. McLane. He looked around to evaluate his companions. Mr. Clarke was bent at the waist, with hands on his knees, and breathing fast. Mistress Clarke's hair was sticking out from all sides of her cap now and her face was flushed. Her quick, short breaths sounded like the bellows Timothy used to encourage flames to catch in his fireplace. Mr. McLane had crumpled down to the ground and sat with his head between his knees as if to hide his face, but he could not prevent gasping. His back heaved up and down.

The Indians wanted to say their prayers. While they were occupied, the four captives huddled together to pray as well. Each with palms together, they made their individual supplications to God. Timothy quietly snorted, *perhaps the Indians are thanking God for their prisoners whilst we, the prisoners, are begging the same God to release us.*

When the Indians finished their invocations, they stood up to remove their belts. The colonists straightened and craned their heads to get a better view. The six Indians pushed something out from the inside of the snakeskins that moments before wrapped around their waists. Then the warriors' conversation erupted into an argument. Harsh words pierced the cold air. As soon as the conversation escalated, it was over. The matter seemed settled. Atian stood up and lobbed what appeared to be stones at them. Timothy caught one and turned it over in his hand. *Biscuits! They are giving us food!*

"Nokehick. Nokehick!"

The prisoners did not care what to call it; they snatched the offering and consumed their portions as if they were born to the wild.

"Was that a parched cornmeal cake?" Mr. McLane asked, looking at Mistress Clarke.

"Yes, I expect it is. If we could have a little more, we would fare better." As Claire said this, she stood and started to walk toward the natives. "Please," she began. Suddenly, Timothy lunged at her and grabbed her arm.

"No! Ye must not beg. Ye MUST not!"

The Indians might not have understood her English word, but they recognized her tone. They reacted to the perceived weakness by puffing out their chests and exchanging looks with furrowed brows. Timothy jerked Mistress Clarke backward as Bezo approached with fury burned in his face. Mr. Clarke rose to circle his protective arms around his wife's shoulders. Mr. McLane's expression registered the fear beating in his chest. To their combined relief, the Indian miraculously changed his mind from whatever foul idea he had in his head and turned to join his brothers.

Before they could rest any longer, they were back on the trail with the small bit of sustenance in their bellies to fuel them. *Am I imagining it, or do I feel better for having had a few small biscuits?*

Tested

The trail was no different from before: low-hanging branches that whipped their arms, brambles that came alive and grabbed at them, and roots that rose up to make them stumble. The sun's rays filtered through the tops of the pines now. Timothy's senses told him they were close to the river. He closed his eyes, lifted his nose skyward, and sniffed the damp air. The lead Indian slowed his steps and came to a halt. Timothy thought he could hear the faint sound of rushing water. Perhaps it was merely the sound of his blood coursing fast and close to his ear drums.

"Contoocook." It was the first time Bezo had addressed Timothy without a commanding tone. The Indian's dark eyes were not jeering or threatening. He sounded like he was stating a fact to a friend.

"Contoocook." Timothy nodded.

"Contoocook!" The Indian said, as if this was a great achievement, and gestured through the trees.

They walked close to four rods on the narrow trail and arrived at a clearing on the bank of the river. The Indians pulled out three small birch-bark canoes concealed under pine boughs. One man retrieved six rough-hewn paddles from the underbrush. Another pulled out three bulky deerskin sacks. A little moan escaped from Timothy's mouth. He saw metal rods sticking out of the sacks. *Now they have rifles!*

Again, Timothy turned to assess the rest of his party. Mr. McLane's face was as red as a cardinal's chest. He was wheezing and his forearm was wet from wiping his brow. Mistress Clarke seemed to have managed well, this time she had stayed clear of the roots. Her cap was askew again, her shawl carried burrs, a few twigs, and brittle leaves, and the thorns had torn her skirt in places. Otherwise, her resolute, upturned chin, reassured Timothy. *She may not be the weakest link after all. Mr. Clarke looks none the worse considering the exercise, but Mr. McLane would be the one to watch.*

The four victims huddled together. Sweat had seeped through the first layer of their clothes, keeping them chilled and shivering during the inactivity.

The unintelligible discourse between the grouped Indians commanded the colonists' attention. *Were they deciding what to do with us?* The dispute was lasting longer than the earlier one and appeared to get heated. *What was it that exercised them so?* Bezo, the one who had taunted him before, seemed insistent with his brethren. He turned several times and nodded in Mr. McLane's direction. *Oh by God's blood, he wants to do away with Mr. McLane! 'Twould be their custom: Eliminate the ones who cannot keep up.*

Atian left the other warriors to walk around the outside circle of the quivering captives. He studied all four of them as he walked, but his look lingered more on Edward McLane.

"Meet his stare with one of yer own. Show no expression. Relax yer face. Measure yer breathing," Timothy said under his breath. Timothy did not dare look at his new comrades to see if they followed his advice, but maintained a steady, relaxed look into the dark eyes of the Indian. The Indian scoffed then rejoined the other Indians.

Timothy glanced at Mr. McLane and felt that he had perhaps passed muster. Mistress Clarke was as straight-backed as a person could be, her shoulders were pressed down, and she had stopped shivering. She took in long, slow breaths of air and exhaled through her nose in such a manner that Timothy could not help but think of a bull about to charge.

"Easy Mistress Clarke, you do not want to give them reason to think you are challenging them."

"Do not worry yourself, Mister Corliss. I will trust in the Lord to get me through. He alone will be my strength, for I am sorely lacking in strength on my own. These verminous savages will not get the best of us," she sniffed.

"With His help we will make the best of a very bad bargain, sir," her husband said, his head a little higher than Timothy had seen before. "'Tis our wish to return and tell of our plight," he said, clenching his teeth.

I fear you are endeavoring to convince yourself more than me, however, 'tis at the very least, a sound attitude. Timothy nodded and curled his lips into a quick smile.

The Indians gestured for them to approach the river where they had positioned the canoes for boarding. The captives obediently fell in line with Timothy in front and Edward McLane at the back; Bezo was close on his heels.

Atian made a sharp gesture while pointing at their feet. "They want us to remove our shoes and boots," Timothy said.

"For goodness sake, what in heaven for? Mr. Clarke asked, looking at Timothy.

"The birch bark is waterproof and strong enough to shoot rapids, but the floor can be easily crushed through." He indicated with a nod of his head to look at the Indians already barefooted.

"Well, 'twill be nice to sit whilst traveling, even if our feet shall get colder," Mistress Clarke said. Encouraged by some hint of positivity, Mr. Clarke acknowledged the attempt with a slight smile and gentle grip of her shoulder.

The sacks were stowed in the rear of the canoes. Atian made another gesture for each to board a different canoe. Timothy raised one foot to get in but then hesitated. *Something is amiss.* The Indian barked a command together with a dramatic sign to board the canoe. Timothy frowned; his eyes darted from one vessel to another. *Ten people in three canoes. Each appeared too small for even three people. How could four people manage with a bulky sack in the back?*

His mind replayed the last image he had of his fellow captives walking toward the river. *Mr. McLane!* Timothy whipped his head around in time to witness the raised tomahawk, poised for a split second over Edward McLane's head. In a tiny span of time, during Edward's final moment on this earth he saw the alarm in Timothy's horrified wide eyes and then registered the disaster that was about to happen. Edward's wool cap was no match for the deadly end of the tomahawk. Edward folded into a heap on the ground; his life's blood draining from his body.

The Clarkes had also seen the horror in Timothy's eyes. They spun around in time to hear the thud and a crack and witness their friend crumble to the ground.

The Indian wasted no time stripping Edward and discarding the clothes to one side. Claire covered her mouth with both hands to keep the cry deep inside her, but it refused to stay down. Henry grabbed his wife under her arms and twisted her away before she could see the Indian disemboweling the unfortunate man as if he was the beaver Timothy had trapped. She buried her head into Henry's chest to muffle the sobbing she could not contain as well as mute the slush of Edward's entrails being born to the light of day. Before Claire buckled, a muffled wail cleansed her lungs and released the last drop of energy she had in her body. Timothy held his breath; he was powerless to move or look away. His brain could not comprehend the images his eyes were sending. It was a degrading death; one that the Indians used to advertise their disdain for weakness.

Timothy was in shock. He was accustomed to performing the same act on animals but had never before witnessed a man gutting another human being. He sank in the middle of the canoe and swallowed hard to keep the bile down. Two Indians boarded the canoe, their copper faces expressionless, as if nothing remarkable had occurred. They sat with Timothy between them. They said nothing. They were naked to the waist again and unaffected by the biting autumn air that stung Timothy's damp cheeks. They dug their paddles deep into the rushing water and pulled into the river; they did not look back; neither did Timothy.

Clouds flitted over the sun that was about three hours high in the afternoon. The Indian in front of Timothy showed no sign of exertion or exhaustion: his strokes were as strong and even as his first stroke. They skirted exposed rocks and avoided downed trees with ease. Timothy willed himself to concentrate on the ropy muscles working on the Indian's lean back with each pull of the paddle. He focused on a tree in the distance and watched it creep closer. He looked for eagles in the sky, squirrels in the trees, deer satisfying their thirst. Anything to block the image . . . and the time passed.

Then, without a word between the paddlers, the canoe veered to the right, and the other two canoes followed. A narrow, sandy area sandwiched between rocks and boulders marked their destination. The

Indians hopped out of their canoes before the birch bottoms could slide along the rough river bottom and motioned to their passengers to do the same.

While donning his boots on the shore, Timothy stole a look at Mistress Clarke. With her husband in a different canoe, he was not sure how she managed without him during the journey. To his relief, she did not cower in the Indians' presence. Her stiff posture and tight lips showed nothing less than firm determination. Henry was at her side as soon as he disembarked and searched her eyes as if reading her soul. Without a word, she gave him a reassuring nod but did not meet his gaze for long.

The Indians removed the sacks and lifted the lightweight canoes up, strapped them to their backs, and carried them inland to a cleared area. This appeared to be a favorite campsite. Several layers of rocks surrounded a fire pit in the center of the clearing. Three conical-shaped structures were about a rod from the pit. They were fashioned with saplings, mud, bark, and leaves. Mounds of hemlock branches, leaves, and moss were piled inside.

The spot was similar to the previous campsite. They chose ones with a slight elevation that made them defensible: The Abenaki had the fierce Mohawks, a branch of the Iroquois, to consider, as well as the English. A copse of trees protected them from the north wind, but unlike the first site, this one had a pleasing view of the river from a bluff. Either these Indians or others had felled enough trees to provide peepholes upstream to the north and to keep many fires burning through the night.

Although not showing any physical sign of succumbing to the low temperature, the Indians casually threw on the warm hide mantles once more. The three remaining captives reeled backward as Atian pulled Edward's frock coat from a sack and put it on over his mantle. He stuck his stomach out and paraded around to imitate Henry's physique and exertion while jogging. The others howled and whooped at the entertainment while they started a fire. Then, as was their custom, their moods instantly changed and they began the praying ritual with their beads.

"Whatever possessed them to . . . ," Claire choked.

"Mr. McLane would have impeded our progress, and there simply was no space for a fourth person in a canoe," Timothy interrupted. "Strive to think of it as a blessing; it was a swift death, and he will not suffer now."

"Ye are referring to the tribulations that await ahead of us, Mr. Corliss. Are ye not? The suffering still to come?" Claire's eyes narrowed.

"We are yet alive, dear Wife. We *shall* return to our blessed children."

"Not *all* our blessed children, Husband!"

"We should be grateful, indeed, that your sister invited our twins to visit them a day longer. Five-year olds would not have managed well either. She saved their lives, and they are waiting for our return."

Claire suddenly clutched the sides of her head. "I

am feeling light-headed. Until I have something in my belly, I fear I shall not be able to stand much longer, let alone endure the remainder of this journey."

Henry and Timothy squeezed against her on either side. Henry cupped a hand over her bent elbow and wrapped an arm around her waist to keep her upright. They walked to a mound of forest bedding protruding from one structure.

"They will not bind us anymore, as they know that no one has followed us thus far. They also have firearms now; any escape on our part would be feckless. Therefore, they might allow us to scavenge for food, perhaps we can find some groundnuts."

"Groundnuts? Pray tell, are they sufficient to sustain us on this wretched journey?" Henry asked.

"Temporarily. We must endeavor to become useful to the savages. If we do what we can to help in some manner, perhaps they will reward us with some food."

"Where can one find groundnuts?" The first prospect of potential food caught Claire's attention.

"Normally in a thicket. I dug up many when I was trapping. Look for a climbing plant. In the autumn one can see brown flowers and bean-like pods hanging on the plant. The tubers grow on thread-like roots, much like potatoes the size of a hen's egg."

The three moved slowly lest their actions be misinterpreted. *No sense in stirring up the Indians' suspicions.* They walked in different directions with digging sticks in hands, heading toward the underbrush. Timothy was the first to find a climbing plant.

"Here, this is one," he called. He lifted the small vine with his stick. He started to dig at its base, but the stick snapped in the hard earth.

The Clarkes had crouched down near Timothy. Although their backs were turned, all three heard the Indian breathing over their shoulders. They turned around at the same time. Henry sucked in a mouthful of air; Claire's eyes grew wide. Timothy put his hand up in defense.

Bezo chuckled. He held a knife in his clenched fist and raised it as if he was going to thrust it into Timothy's back. Instead, he knelt down and plunged it into the ground. He stabbed the cold earth multiple times with the same intensity as if he was murdering an enemy. His blade scooped around until he produced three groundnuts. He dropped them in front of Claire who quickly passed one each to the others. She used her hands to brush off the dirt and then devoured her tuber, barely chewing. It had a woody, bitter taste.

"They are better boiled or fried in fat, but in this moment, I care not a button," Timothy said and popped his in his mouth.

"Hobbenis," the Indian nodded. He spread his arms wide, smiled, and twisted at the waist while looking around. "Hobbenis."

"I expect this must be a good area for groundnuts," Henry said, mildly amused by the Indian's dramatic gesture. "I see their attitude toward us varies moment to moment. We are met with either favor or frowns; then one may quickly evolve into the other."

Claire and Timothy had already left Henry's side and were busy searching for more climbing vines. With Henry's help, they were rewarded for their efforts, but did not find enough to fill up the entire vacancy in their stomachs. They had to be content watching their masters pull out more nokehick from the hollow of their belts and hope they would once again share. But they did not. The smell of the parched corn cakes frying in beaver fat over the open flame was as tantalizing as the aroma of venison haunches roasting on their home fires.

As the sun moved lower and was about to disappear, the three followed the Indians' lead and fortified a tepee inside and out with fresh hemlock branches on top of the withered ones. After shoring up nature's roof and bedding, they crawled inside and attempted to push harsh images out of their dreams. Each found the attempt difficult and slept in fits and starts, at best. Wolves howled to defend their territory from other wolves, owls hooted from one tree to another, and an unidentified creature sniffed outside their shelter.

The dawn was long in coming but brought a warmer start to the day. Under different circumstances, the emerging sun's light would be a lift to spirits dampened by the short, near winter days. Claire surfaced from the makeshift abode and whispered in a monotone, "Thanks be to God for the sun in the sky on this morn," as if her mouth had no connection with her heart. The three followed the Indians, helped them with the canoes, and without any reminder, took off their footwear, and silently climbed in.

Timothy wished he could yell to his companions as they passed Sugar Ball Island at the junction of the Contoocook and Merrimac Rivers. On this very island Hannah Dustin and Timothy's kin, Mary Corliss Neff, put an end to their captivity and winter march in 1697, almost fifty years earlier. Hannah proved to the General Court in Boston that their ordeal was not invented when she presented them with ten Indian scalps she had severed from their heads, an Indian rifle, and a tomahawk. *Those brave goodwives of the past give me hope. Would that I could possess some of their bravery.*

The Merrimac, or Morodemak as the Indians called it, was wider than the Contoocook and presented several hazards to the canoes. The Indians sliced through the bone-chilling water in zigzags in an effort to avoid rocks and floating debris. When the obstruction was too difficult to avoid, the group portaged the canoes until they passed the hazard. The exercise taxed the little strength the captives had. When they carried the canoes over the rugged terrain, Timothy heard the Clarkes' grunting, which verified they were as spent as he was.

Timothy was a lot colder when back in the canoe just sitting after the exercise. His mind started to wander. *'Twould take but a moment to perish in this water if such dangers cause us to capsize. Perhaps, it would be a merciful death . . . but would not a hatchet to the head be quicker? I must endeavor to train my mind to wander to more pleasant thoughts. Ah, but is not the end to this nightmare a pleasant thought?* Timothy's chest filled with air and then fell with the sudden expiration. *It will be getting a lot colder soon.* He wrapped his arms around himself thinking of the coming winter.

As the days stretched out, the six Indians and three white people slowly made their way toward the Connecticut River. Each colonist drew upon whatever measure of strength it would take to endure: The Clarkes were in constant prayer and anxious to return to their children while Timothy concerned himself with his father, mother, and brothers. *How must they be faring without me?*

Throughout their tribulation, Atian had offered some relief from their discomfort: Fir balsam salve eased frozen hands and feet; tea from oak bark and a poultice made from ash bark and comfrey leaves healed scratches and cuts. The Indians addressed the suffering on the outside of their bodies, but not always the inside: Stomachs continued to complain. If the Indians shared anything, it was only the discarded parts: entrails, ears, old bones.

As they headed northward, the groundnuts were harder to find; Timothy and the Clarkes were close to starving. They had to substitute bark for the tubers. The Indians had not shared any sustenance for several days despite their successful hunting and trapping forays and small raids on villagers' barns.

Finally, one day after inspecting the hostages, the Indians must have worried their captives would starve before making it to Canada, and if dead they would not receive any compensation at all for them. Atian rifled through the contents of his sack; he got Henry's attention and tossed him a pair of horse hooves. Henry examined them; he exchanged baffled looks with his wife, who curled her lips in disgust and frowned at the strange token.

"Forget what they are and where they came from. We can boil them and drink the broth. They are offering us a pot and space at the fire," Timothy pointed to Atian, smiling with his chest puffed out as if he had just gifted them a fattened pig to roast. "We must show thanks for the gift." He returned the Indian's smile with one of his own and nodded in appreciation. The Clarkes followed suit and scrambled to the beckoning native, who was holding the pot in his outstretched hand.

The trails were the main routes of the fur trade and Indians of all tribes and clans traveled them; they knew them as well as Timothy knew the trails around Haverhill, although these covered a much larger territory. The Indians pressed the exhausted captives into a quick pace, making a rest to catch their breaths impossible, especially when they drew closer to white settlements. At those locations, searching for food was out of the question; without fuel for their bodies, their stamina was severely compromised. It was not unusual for one of them to trip and remain sprawled on the ground until an Indian's swift kick prompted them to continue on.

When they had to travel on land, the six Indians always maintained a quick pace. When deep, fresh snow covered the trail, the Indians strapped on well-constructed snowshoes that packed down the snow and made the course a little easier for their captives.

The terrifying reality of their abductions had abated somewhat. The three fell into a state of guarded acceptance, most of the time moving as if under a spell. They did nothing on purpose to antagonize their captors and endeavored to pitch in whenever the situation warranted it. Life settled into a monotonous routine—one that consisted of constant movement, constant cold, and constant hunger.

Days stretched into weeks. Timothy was weary. He and the others had endured days and nights of rain, snow, and ice. They did not always have the luxury of sleeping in well-built shelters or caves. Burrowing inside a hollowed dead log or tucked under a canoe was the best they could hope for at times. When God was merciful and saw that they had just about reached the extent of their resilience, He answered their prayers with flashes of sunlight through the trees and blue patches that emerged from behind wispy clouds. On those occasions, the sun melted the snow and warmed their bodies, if not their spirits. But then, their new adversary became the icy slush they had to plod through.

In the six weeks they had been on the move since the Contoocook River, they had traveled northwest through unsettled territory, across the rocky Sunapee Lake, and up the Connecticut River, the Wells River, and down the Winooski River to Lake Champlain. The greatest challenge to their endurance, next to constant hunger, was portaging between waterways. They had all lost weight, their tattered clothing allowed cold air to reach exposed skin, and their bodies were slow and weak from weariness; they did not need the extra weight of a canoe, no matter how light, pushing down on them as well. Their composure was challenged every time an Indian shrieked when a branch scratched along the fragile side of a canoe on the narrow trails.

At the northern end of Lake Champlain in Canada they took the Iroquois River where, much to the relief of the captives, the Indians let them fish and allowed them to fry what they caught.

"Namossack kesos," one Indian had said spreading his arms as if showing off the river and then mimed eating a fish.

"'Twould not be any surprise if their generosity stemmed from trying to make us more acceptable to our future French masters." Timothy said while stuffing a piece of fish in his mouth and sucking his fingers.

"At this moment, I am not bothered in the least with their reason. This is the most delicious fish that has ever passed between my lips!" Henry said closing his eyes in ecstasy.

"Careful not to swallow any bones in your rush to placate your belly!" Claire said in between chewing. Her eyes smiled at her husband, the first sign of pleasure during the hundreds of miles they'd traveled. Timothy could not help but grin at Henry.

Whether it was because their stomachs were not complaining or the full moon was smiling on them, or perhaps it was because the temperature was more pleasing, the Clarkes began to relax. Timothy thought he was hearing things when something sounding like laughter drew his attention.

"There, my dear Mr. Clarke, the Big Dipper. Right there! Tell me you see it now!" Claire pointed skyward and chuckled as her husband pretended he did not see the constellation. "Are ye daft, Husband?"

"Daft? Why yes, I believe I am!" and he pulled her closer to him.

Timothy smiled. His friends were enjoying a small pocket of peace. *These rare moments have to be savored.*

From Bad to Worse

"That's right, wrap the ball into the piece of cloth. It will serve to keep the ball inside when you tilt the gun." Timothy's father stood off to the side and continued giving his son instructions, even though Timothy knew full well the workings of his new rifle.

Timothy raised the gun and pushed the butt into his right shoulder with his cheek barely resting on the maple wood. He steadied the long shaft with his left hand while pivoting with his right foot and stepping forward with his left, giving his upper body a slight twist. Choosing a low-hanging branch, he aimed, held his breath, and pulled the cock back. Timothy fired; smoke blinded his eyes. He heard the branch crack and fall. A grin spread across his face as he glanced back at his father.

"Father?" He was confused. He squinted to see through the smoke, but daylight had changed to the semi-darkness of dawn. Timothy sat up on his elbows and blinked. Why had his father painted his face? But it was not his father's face. This face was threatening: A bottom lip jutted out with its corners stretched downward. He was now inches away from Timothy's head and the frightened young man read hatred in the strange Indian's black eyes under the deep furrowed forehead. This unfamiliar figure bent down lower; greasy black braids swung to and fro. His breath was warm on Timothy's face. Red-painted stripes ran the length of his hairless torso. He was yelling a different sounding gibberish than Timothy was accustomed to hearing. He grabbed Timothy with one hand and yanked him off the evergreen and moss bedding. *He's going to scalp me!*

Timothy looked over the Mohawk Indian's shoulder to see a familiar scar-faced Abenaki charging at them with his tomahawk raised over his head and gripped in two hands. In a split second, the Mohawk's menacing expression distorted as his head almost split in half in front of Timothy. Timothy fell to his knees and snapped his head to the left to avoid the scarlet spray, but the warm gush of blood and brains caught his right cheek and shoulder. Bezo smiled and gave a quick nod at Timothy before running back to the melee.

The Clarkes clung to each other, trembling, and with wide eyes that radiated fear. Timothy crawled over to them. The fierce battle playing out before his eyes was oddly mesmerizing: Indian against Indian, all formidable warriors, fighting to the death. *I have a suspicion we are the prize.* A weird sensation came over him. For the first time since his capture, he found himself on the Abenakis' side. He gasped as Atian fell to the ground. The brave warrior did not issue a sound as a Mohawk's tomahawk lodged in his chest.

Timothy felt himself jerked off the ground and roughly pushed back to stand next to Henry. More gibberish. The Mohawk's arms were beating as if he were an eagle about to take flight. The remaining Indians continued their savagery as the single Mohawk herded them toward the river. The Indian sliced the air with his hatchet to hasten them. They quickly carried three canoes into the water, took off their footwear, and each knelt in a different vessel as commanded. The Mohawk quickly put a rope with a slip knot around Timothy's head and attached it to a strip of rawhide around Timothy's ankles behind him. He did the same to Henry. The Indian rolled himself in the stern of Claire's canoe with her at the bow. The Indian threw a paddle at each man. Henry caught his and held it at arm's length over the gunwale.

"I have no training with this sort of thing," Henry yelled to Timothy. "What shall I do?"

"'Tis simple, Henry," Timothy responded over his shoulder as he dug in the water. Stay behind me and do everything I do. Do your best to keep up! This Mohawk will sink your canoe if ye do not! I wager this fellow will try to put a lot of distance between ourselves and the Abenakis as quickly as he can—if any of them survive. We are currency to the Abenakis and they will not give us up so easily."

They paddled several miles up the Iroquois River, passing the first of four French forts on the river, Fort Richelieu, which later gave its name to the river. Timothy tried several times to shift his weight off his aching feet, but he only succeeded in tightening the noose around his neck. The rapids challenged his ability to steer and not pull on his constraints. Finally, the Mohawk paddled out to their right and pointed to a clearing ahead.

The Indian cut the rawhide off the prisoners' ankles but held the ropes connecting the men's nooses. As he got out of the canoe, Timothy tried to read the passive expression of the Indian but knew it was futile. The two men carried the canoes under the threatening posture of the Indian, away from the stony beach and climbed up a path to a throng of wild-eyed Mohawk Indians that did everything but smack their lips upon laying eyes on the three white people.

The Indians bobbed their heads at their fellow Mohawk and seemed to be congratulating him with their hooting and hollering. A frightening, festive feel rose in the air, and an excited energy mounted in the natives as they surrounded the three anxious prisoners. Drums were beating in the background. The Indians pushed them along amid the varied gleeful and harsh sounds of another tongue they did not know. They were herded toward a shelter bearing a construction and design similar to that of the Abenaki Indians: long strips of bark and animal skins covering the cone-shaped frame. Before entering, Timothy thought he could see a cluster of white people inside another structure. A middle-aged squaw held open a deerskin flap; her fluttering hand motioned for them to go inside. Her braided hair was powdered and she had painted her face with red and yellow designs. Carved bracelets clacked as her impatient hand repeated the command. The jewels in her earlobes jiggled as her head nodded in unison with her hand. The squaw closed the animal flap behind her; the excited yelling outside filtered through and rose in intensity with the rhythmic drum beating. *'Tis becoming more frenetic with each passing minute.* The harrowing sounds went through to Timothy's very core.

The same Indian that had fought the Abenakis entered, removed the rope from around Henry's and Timothy's necks, and left.

Timothy sat facing Henry and Claire and burned his eyes into theirs. He put one hand on one shoulder of each friend and gave a slight squeeze. "What happens next may be the hardest part of the whole journey. We have survived a horrible trial over the last weeks that perhaps has prepared us for this moment. Ye *must* be strong. Ye *must* think of the future and those waiting for you at home."

"Mister Corliss, what do you mean? You are correct, we have survived to make it thus far. But you yourself spoke of the French taking us into servitude. That cannot be nearly as bad as what we have endured."

"Can ye not comprehend? We are not in the

Abenakis' control anymore but their fierce enemies, the Mohawk. They make the Abenakis look gentle in comparison. They do not have the same alliance with the French. They exist separate from all others. I fear . . . I fear we may be forced to run a gauntlet."

"Gauntlet?" Henry's eyes grew wide and he looked at his wife. "What is your meaning, gauntlet?"

"Ye *must not* be the last to cross the line, nor is it the time to be demure. I tell ye honestly what it is that I know to be true from those who witnessed and participated in such a thing. If I am correct, we shall be stripped of our clothing and made to run a distance while the women of the tribe attempt to burn us with torches. 'Tis a game they take great delight in."

"Lord have mercy!"

"You said we should take care not to be last?" Claire's eyes harbored the fear growing inside her.

"Ye shall meet an ungodly end that will succeed in making our entire journey up to this point a lovely sojourn." Timothy paused, wondering if he should continue or reveal the wretched plan. *Best to tell them so they may use the knowledge to their advantage somehow.* "All the torches shall come together and circle the unfortunate one or ones who shall become a toy to tease and provoke with the fire. When the game is done," he looked them squarely in the eyes and whispered, "nothing shall remain of the person but embers."

"Claire!" Henry hugged his wife close.

"I am certain I saw white people inside another

hut. We will not be competing with just ourselves."

From outside, a hand pulled up the door flap. The three sat motionless and silent staring at the Indian entering and wondering what would happen next—but afraid to know for sure. The noise of increasing fervor and commotion outside assaulted their ears; the wave of smoke assaulted their nostrils.

Timothy had never seen a sachem, but the solemn man standing before him had the quiet dignity of a leader. His head was shaved with the exception of a row of hair about half a finger high down the middle of his skull. The feathers that had been jabbed into the tuft stuck out at all angles. He wore bone earrings and a necklace laced with bear claws and beads hung down his broad russet chest. Red material draped over his bare shoulders and hung close to the ground. Four squaws stood reverently behind him. The reserved demeanor of the small group of Indians facing them was in direct contrast to the conduct of their fellow Indians outside dancing and screaming like seagulls.

"We eat now," he said in perfect English, startling the three captives, and motioned to follow him to a fire pit. They read nothing in his inscrutable expression. The squaws positioned themselves behind Timothy and the Clarkes to steer them; seeing the determination in the women's faces, they complied.

Had they been ignorant of the Indians' barbaric practice, the roasted chunks of bear meat and fish baked on flat rocks would have slid down their throats much easier. Each of the three struggled to finish what had been laid before them, chewing the meat longer than necessary and with heads bowed to make frantic supplications to God. The realization that the sachem had some working knowledge of English added to their discomfort. They did not dare speak to each other. Not knowing what to say to the chief under the strange circumstance produced an awkward silence that the sachem might have promoted. Meanwhile, the squaws chirped among themselves and punctuated their chatter with bursts of laughter.

When the sachem was satisfied, he rose. The squaws took his cue and motioned to Timothy and the Clarkes to rise as well. The women ushered the three outside toward the cheering crowd. Many wore expectant faces as if they were eager to be entertained. Several of the squaws had long torches that they slammed against the earth in unison with the drumming and amid the caterwauling of the others. Timothy had never experienced a fervor of this intensity before. He hesitated before the wild-eyed savages with their hideous grimaces and hoped this macabre setting would not be the last sight of his short life. His tongue ran along his dry lips and teeth.

"Go to them," the sachem said and pointed to the group of about twenty huddled colonists whom Timothy had noticed before.

"Mistress Clarke! Mister Clarke!" two gaunt ladies stumbled out from the assembly, their filthy clothes torn and shredded along their cuffs and hems but their sunken eyes wide with happiness to be reunited for a brief moment with a taste of home. The Clarkes stood still, slack-jawed, and stared at the shadows of friends they once knew, not believing whom they were seeing. Suddenly, Claire rushed forward and all but threw herself at them; she flung her arms around the two ladies, her hands nearly meeting behind their backs, and pulled them into her.

"'Tis really you, Mistress Lewis! Mistress Duncan! When they separated us, I thought ye had been . . ."

"No, they chose to keep some of us alive but we lost my brother," Mistress Lewis looked at her sister-in-law, "and my dear husband as well as Mistress Leonard and the little ones that could not keep up." Tears threatened to spill out, but she wiped them out of her eyes with the side of a dirty finger.

"These Indians attacked our group and stole us from the Abenakis two days ago," Mistress Duncan said.

Claire nodded and said, "I fear we have had the same plight." She looked at Henry and Timothy as if to ask, should I tell them about the gauntlet? Henry shook his head.

The relief of seeing their friends again since enduring the pressure of captivity brought about an emotional release that Timothy feared would attract attention. *It could lead to a dangerous level of hysterics, and the Mohawks held the loss of control over one's emotions in less regard than the Abenakis.* As Claire started to slump and shake, Henry held her up.

"Please, mistress. You must *not* cry. Hold yourself

together!" Timothy whispered.

Claire nodded. She inhaled a cleansing breath, but maintained a firm grip on her friends' shoulders with the desperation of one trying to hold onto a happier past. Henry grabbed one of his wife's hands, spun her to face him, and with both of his hands sandwiching hers like he was about to pray, he bore into her eyes. "Be strong, dear Wife, as shall I. Pray to our dear Lord."

The captives waited for a lifetime, listening to the fevered pitch of the crazed Indians and the monotonous drumming on the animal skins. The sounds grew too loud to converse anymore. Just when he thought he would start screaming himself, Timothy recognized the squaw that had opened the flap to the shelter standing before the colonists. She was ordering them to do something. Getting no reaction, she barked the command over and over and pulled at the colonists' clothing nearest to her. The group responded with cries of resistance and frightened voices. Only when threatened with the squaws' flaming torches did the captives' trembling hands start to remove their clothing.

"Mr. Clarke, Mistress Clarke, stay in the middle of the pack. If ye venture to the sides, their torches will find ye," Timothy hissed, "and by God's blood do not fall!"

Three squaws used their torches to move the shivering, naked colonists, like animals being herded, toward the middle of two lines of hysterical squaws banging their outstretched poles against the ground.

The light cast from the dancing flames made their contorted, painted faces gruesome. People were tripping and falling as the front of the pack hesitated to face the jeering gauntlet, but the back pushed to avoid the torches coming at them from behind.

In the maelstrom, screams of pain and agony mixed with the piercing squeals as the squaws reached their targets with their blazing torches. The ball of panicked colonists tightened and picked up speed. People gasped for breath that fear had stolen as a smell of burning flesh wrapped around them. Timothy's pulse thumped wildly in his throat. The ball began to change shape as some chose to run and get beyond the torch-carrying squaws and some fell or limped from the searing pain.

Timothy and the Clarkes ran together. As Timothy advised, they stuck to their positions in the middle of the pack. Claire was in the dead center. Their eyes focused on the person in front to avoid the demons in the squaws' eyes. The sachem was standing somewhere ahead of them, marking the end of the atrocious race.

"Concentrate on reaching the sachem. We can make it!" Henry said and then let out a bone-chilling cry. Burnt flesh pricked Timothy's nostrils. Henry wrapped his right arm across his chest and faltered a step.

"Henry! Oh dear Husband!" Claire yanked on Henry's left arm to pull him away from another assault. The flame grazed his back.

A hand reached out and pushed Timothy to the left. He lost the protection of two shields. He was exposed. He looked over to see a squaw, whose ghastly, jeering face would haunt him forever after in his dreams, aiming her torch at his thigh. She ran at him. He measured two strides between himself and the two people in front of him. He needed to squeeze between them. His right leg stretched out to pull himself forward. Before his left leg could extend, the torch found it. The excruciating pain caused him to stumble. He reeled in a circle and ran into another runner who was on the receiving end of the squaw's second round. The man's yelp was lost among the other agonizing cries.

Timothy reached the sachem limping and hopping like many of the animals he had wounded. If a fellow colonist had been standing there, he would have fallen into his arms. The sachem stood erect and still, only his eyes moved, scanning the horrific scene as one would take in a nondescript view of the land: His dour expression neither showed his heart's distaste nor joy.

The torches were no longer a threat. Timothy bent at the waist and held onto his knees for support as he worked to gain his breath. His thigh screamed in pain and begged for his complete attention. Others joined him whose prayers God chose to answer favorably—for now. Some were unscathed; others were inspecting their burns and wincing. Timothy stood and craned his head around the new arrivals to look for the Clarkes. He recognized the two ladies the Clarkes had joyfully greeted a mere ten minutes earlier. They suffered several burns between them but managed to cross the invisible line upright. Two women and a man crawled to the finish. Timothy did not see any sign of the Clarkes around him or among those staggering to the finish.

The merciless squaws had bunched themselves around a common target and were torturing the miserable victim or victims amid their ear-splitting shrieks. The tormentors blocked Timothy's view and made it impossible to identify the wretched souls. *Are they . . .* suddenly, his mouth watered and he tasted salt. His stomach heaved. He bent at the waist again, this time to expel the remains of his last meal.

A Familiar Face

"**M**r. Corliss!" He heard Mistress Clarke's voice and peered up to see her as well as Mr. Clarke, contorting in pain, but very much safe. She did not appear to be concerned with any burns herself: She was among the lucky ones. Although he knew the games were not over yet.

"Praise the Lord. Ye both are here!" Timothy gasped.

"Our clothes. They have our clothes in a pile," Claire said, pointing to a small mountain of ragged and dirty material. They rummaged through it, quickly snatching anything that resembled what they had taken off earlier. The injured gingerly eased the loose clothing over their wounds. Timothy did not dare pull on breeches that would cause further torment but selected a long tunic.

The Mohawks' full attention was now on the miserable figures writhing on the ground and screaming for mercy. The drums were beating faster. The colonists' absorption was divided between trying to ease their own pain and hoping for a swift end to the ghastly devastation playing out too close to their ears. They neither saw nor heard the intruder sneaking up from the river.

Henry and Claire were standing on the outside edge of the group of colonists. Some were standing, but others had slumped to the ground in various postures depending on their injuries. The Clarkes had turned their backs on the sickening spectacle, but they could not ignore the smell of burning flesh crawling into their nostrils or the sound of agonized wailing from someone in unspeakable pain. Timothy, horrified that he was utterly helpless to stop the misery, willed himself to concentrate on the burn on his leg. Henry was the first to see the scar-faced Abenaki crouched under a hemlock and motioning them to follow. Henry elbowed Timothy and nodded in the Indian's direction. Claire took in a short breath of surprise, covered her mouth, and quickly looked right and left, to be sure the Abenaki had not drawn the Mohawks' or the colonists' attention.

"I suppose he is the better of two evils. Claire, go first; go slow so as not to draw suspicion," Henry whispered close to her ear.

"What about Mistresses Lewis and Duncan? We must find them," she whispered back. Her head cocked to the side and she gave Timothy and her husband an imploring look, but she already guessed what Timothy was going to say.

He gave a short shake of his head, "If ye want to get out alive, this is the only way—more people sneaking away would assuredly draw attention to us. Also, we do not know how many canoes are ready for us down there."

The Abenaki was scooping air toward himself as if to pull the three to him. The departure would have to be soon or he would be in danger as well.

"Keep your head down, go slow, and appear to be inspecting a burn as you walk," Timothy said. "Mr. Clarke, ye go next."

The Abenaki led Claire to the river. Henry made it as far as the hemlock where he had noticed Bezo. Timothy was about to take his first step. Suddenly, a chill ran down Timothy's spine as he heard Mistress Duncan calling over to Henry.

"Mister Clarke! Where is your wife? Is she faring well?"

Mistress Duncan was a slight woman with a birdlike chirp to her voice that others dominated easily in a conversation; however, on this day and this moment, it seemed her voice acquired a deep intensity it did not have before. Her words took flight over the moaning and weeping as if an orator in front of an angry mob had uttered them. Timothy turned to stone. Henry glanced over his shoulder but escaped into the thick pines. Mistress Duncan hobbled after him.

"Mister Clarke!"

Timothy watched as a nearby squaw stopped, dropped her heavy bundle of firewood, and looked around. At first she did not see Mistress Duncan, but on her second scan of the throng, she saw the woman staggering toward the forest. *She must think the woman is trying to escape. God's blood! I have to act fast! She is going to alert the whole tribe!*

The squaw opened her mouth at the same time the rest of the Mohawks' howling and screeching reached an unnerving crescendo. Her voice mingled with the cacophony and dissipated. Her smothered alarm did not reach the Indians' ears to tear them away from the focus of their attention: The morbid delight in burning their victims.

Timothy sidestepped around the outside of the bunched colonists. He hid behind the ones standing, as if they were shields, in case the squaw noticed him as well. He peered around a couple clutching each other and weeping. Mistress Duncan was almost at the hemlock. Unbeknownst to her, the squaw was after her like a cat after a mouse.

At just the right time, Mistress Duncan's sister-in-law, Mistress Lewis, on the opposite side of the group from Timothy, screamed to her, "Sister! Help me! No! Take your hands off me! Help! Margaret!" A squaw, sporting a maniacal smirk, was dragging Mistress Lewis along the ground while another was pushing her from behind.

Mistress Duncan heard her name above the din and turned around. The squaw galloping toward her had grasped a stick and was waving her arms like she was having a tantrum. Margaret Duncan reeled backward.

She raised her arms in self-defense and buckled. Her mind immediately erased any concern she had about Mr. Clarke. Timothy gaped as the poor woman was yanked back into the melee where her sister-in-law, Mistress Lewis, was being dragged. Guilt washed through his mind: He was torn between running to her aid and making haste to escape. He bit his bottom lip. He concluded that together they could not make it out alive. His eyes swept the scene and noticed no one was watching him as he inched away from one captivity and back toward another. He may be escaping this hell but would still be a captive in a yet uncertain future.

As he half ran and limped on the steep, narrow path, he muttered a quick prayer for the brethren he left behind. *May they survive—but if not, may their deaths be quick and their souls find mercy in heaven.*

No canoes! Bezo and the Clarkes were gone! He splashed into the river up to his knees and looked up and down. Timothy saw the two canoes gaining distance from him, but he could not risk yelling. He looked down at the ground and held his forehead; he didn't have a plan. *Lord have mercy on me if the Mohawks find me! And they shall soon enough.*

A whistle! His heart beat faster. He whirled around. Under a thicket of brush hanging over the water was a canoe with two squaws waiting for him. They stroked over to him and commanded something in their tongue. He flung himself into the canoe, causing it to rock precariously amid the squaws' recriminations as they tried to balance their vessel. Then, both leaned forward and dug into the water with such vehemence that Timothy was flung backward.

Like the males in the tribe, the women wore a minimal amount of clothing to allow for full arm movement. A flap of deerskin secured at the neck covered their nakedness in the front, but their backs were bare. Timothy noticed sweat glistening on the back of the squaw in front of him, yet, like the warriors, she showed no sign of fatigue and maintained strong and rhythmic pulls of her paddle.

They were about five minutes out when Timothy felt the tip of a paddle poking him in the back. He twisted around to determine if this was meant as ridicule but noticed the squaw was offering him something in a covered baked-clay bowl. She nodded, made a motion for him to drink, and resumed paddling with increased intensity to make up for the seconds her partner was doing all the work. She was not unpleasant looking and her encouraging smile made her eyes crinkle at the edges. Hesitant to trust her, Timothy frowned and stared at the bowl. She took one hand off the paddle and flapped it at him, signaling urgency and uttering gibberish. Timothy relented and sipped the cooled tea made from willow bark, echinacea, and rose hips. It would fight infection as well as deaden the pain and reduce inflammation.

His scorched leg commanded his attention again. The linen tunic he had grabbed from the pile of clothes was not long enough to protect his burn from the sun and air. It was red and swollen, and blisters were forming. To ease the pain a little, he stretched his leg out on the side of the canoe and adjusted his weight to counterbalance the difference. He used his hands to make a shadow over the burn.

The squaw tapped his shoulder again with her paddle. She was about his age, much younger than the squaw in the bow. She reached in a sack and produced another earthen pot containing a gooey substance. She signed putting the salve on his burn. After wincing at the first contact, he dropped the sticky dollops liberally over the site. He caught the runaway drips with his index finger and sucked them off. *Honey sweetened the bitter chokecherries—it tastes quite good. It's commencing to feel a bit better, too.*

The burbling, small tributaries along the river's edge combined with the steady push of the canoe. It was all very soothing. Perhaps the tea and comforting salve had more influence. He made circles with his shoulders and relaxed his muscles. He bent his head to the right and left and felt the tenseness leave his neck. Then the miniature whirlpools the squaw's paddle formed and pushed down the side of the canoe locked him in a trance.

Timothy's chin was resting on his chest when he noticed a change in the canoe's direction. The women made a sharp turn and headed for shore. He jerked his head up and opened his eyes. The rocky coast offered no sign of a beach or a path. The squaws put their paddles down and slipped off from opposite sides into the waist-high water. The older one gestured for

Timothy to stay while they walked the canoe to more shallow water, close to the rocks. They steadied the canoe and nodded. Gingerly, Timothy eased himself out of the canoe. The younger squaw climbed up on a rock while her friend pushed down on the stern to raise the bow. Like partners well-attuned to a task, they silently went about lifting the canoe over the rocks.

With great effort, Timothy followed the women and maneuvered up the obstacle. He grimaced with each stretch of his skin on his damaged leg.

Invisible from the river and protected from Mohawk eyes was a cache of canoes, some made of birch bark and a few resembling burned-out logs. They were neatly hidden behind several large granite rocks. The women stored the canoe with the others and hid the paddles elsewhere. The younger one motioned for Timothy to follow. It wasn't until they had ducked under some low-hanging branches that he was finally able to discern a path that wound up a small hill. *A Mohawk would never know the path is here unless he came this close.*

An Indian was stationed by a rock outcropping at the summit. He nodded to the squaws and stared emotionless as Timothy passed. They continued on through a small wooded section until they came to a tall fence with vertical poles mudded and lashed together. They had arrived at an Abenaki settlement. *The Mohawks would be foolish to attack the Abenakis here, as protected as they are, and with the number of French forts up and down the river. But the proud and vengeful Mohawks are known to retaliate with ferocity and Bezo's group has wiped out the small band that attacked them. The Mohawks may seek retribution.*

"Mr. Corliss! What a relief to see you!" Henry greeted him inside the fence wearing a tunic, deerskin leggings, and an animal hide over one bare shoulder. Timothy could almost count his ribs. Henry's bare arm had a bulge, covered with a woven cloth, the spot where the torch had met his flesh. Another strip of plant cloth stretched under his armpits to secure a second dressing on his back. Timothy was about to ask about the dressings when he saw Henry's wife, equally happy to see him again.

"Did you see my friends," she hesitated, "before you left?" She dared not look Timothy in the eye and regretted asking for fear the answer would confirm her suspicions.

"When I departed they were both alive."

She closed her eyes and sighed. Timothy had tried to sound hopeful but his voice lacked authority. Her downcast look told him she was not wholly comforted.

Timothy scrutinized the Abenaki village. It consisted of ten wooden longhouses erected on the edge of a circle. Seasoned bark over wooden frames covered the rounded tops and sides. The middle section of one side could be exposed when the summer heat became oppressive. There were openings at each end for more ventilation. A few dome-shaped wigwams and huts were scattered about a grassy, cleared area. Children, mostly boys, were playing a game with a ball and stick and ducking around the structures. One almost collided with a squaw carrying a heavy sack. Timothy smiled at their antics. He noticed beyond them there was another gate at the far end of the settlement.

The young squaw interrupted his inspection; she approached with a strong and regal-looking man. The Indian wore a ground-length cloak woven with plant fibers that was secured in front with a sharpened stick. Like the other Indian chief Timothy had seen, the man was bare chested. *Do they not feel the bite of the winter wind?* Round bone earrings attached to a necklace of the same design stretched his earlobes down an inch. White hair showed under a peaked birch-bark hood with large flaps that draped over his shoulders like a mantle and feathers stuck sideways in the tip. His wrinkled, bronzed face did not match the well-proportioned, straight-backed frame: It was as if someone had placed his head on a younger man's body.

"Sachem," the young woman said as introduction, "Tomasus."

Timothy and the Clarkes nodded respectfully in his direction. Tomasus crossed his arms over his chest, spaced his legs, and studied the three of them for an uncomfortable period.

Finally, he cleared his throat, but it sounded more like a growl, and said in English, "Mohawks are bad. They killed five good warriors. You are safe here. We wait. I send my messengers for your ransom. How much are you worth?"

Timothy was taken aback with the man's abruptness. When the surprise of his candor cleared, he felt the words sticking in his throat. *If I say too small a sum, they may kill me or sell me right away. If I say too much, father will not be able to pay it.* His tongue ran along his front teeth.

"Your English is very good, Tomasus." Timothy needed time to think.

"My father said English and French make a sachem strong, so I learned when I was young from many Jesuit priests that visited our village. Our numbers were great then. We have lost too many to war and sickness." Tomasus offered no other comment but stared at Timothy until he answered his question.

"Twenty shillings?" Timothy immediately regretted not sounding more confident.

He turned to the Clarkes with a questioning arch of his brows. "The same," Henry spoke up.

"If ransom is no good, we trade you to Frenchmen." Tomasus's tone showed no emotion. He studied each one and Timothy questioned if the chief was evaluating his chances with the French or, perhaps, pondering if they could be good replacements for the warriors the tribe lost. Then, he addressed the squaw he called Olidaha. Before he left the uneasy hostages, he spoke several minutes with Olidaha in their tongue. She nodded in agreement and beckoned the three to follow her.

"Was twenty shillings enough?" Timothy turned to ask Henry while he maintained Olidaha's brisk pace.

"If it is not, Claire and I are in a peck of trouble. There are two of us!" Henry replied.

Village Life

*T*he squaw guided them to one of the longhouses and signed to them to go inside. The smooth-packed dirt comforted Timothy's bare feet. In spite of the size of the building, there was a warm, cozy atmosphere. A dozen cooking fires ran the length of one side. Smoke holes above them had flaps and could close when it rained or snowed. Mothers and daughters occupied all positions in front of the cooking fires. Girls five years and younger were playing nearby with corn husk dolls or tending to younger siblings while their older sisters helped their mothers with the cooking. On the opposite side, animal skins covered low platforms where the families slept. Above the beds, shelves hung for storage. Timothy scanned the living quarters. *About a dozen families live here together.*

The animated interactions between the older squaws and the mothers with their daughters gave the interior a light-hearted atmosphere that intrigued the three white people. They seemed more jovial doing their tasks than the women back home. The captives followed their guide down the center of the expanse, and the conversations began to hush as each squaw became aware of the strangers in the longhouse. Most of the children and many of the squaws had never seen white people. Hands froze; eyes watched. The younger children came closer to inspect them. Olidaha spoke to the group; her words must have addressed their curiosity: They resumed their tasks, but they continued in silence, stealing furtive glances over their shoulders. The youngest children cocked their heads to the side and remained transfixed.

The older squaw that had rescued Timothy entered carrying a small container with more salve and a bowl of the special tea that Timothy drank in the canoe. Her dark, leathery skin was tinged with a rosy hue. This one was all about business; her eyes didn't smile like Olidaha's. She motioned for Timothy to sit and drink the tea. Then she proceeded to apply the gooey salve to his thigh and topped it off with dried sphagnum moss that the squaws collected from the swampy coastal area and dried. Its antiseptic qualities inhibited bacterial growth while absorbing pus and blood. He winced as she wrapped a strip of woven material gently over the moss and around his leg.

"I deduce we may be attracting some flies with all that honey before too long," Henry smiled. He lowered his head; a bad memory flittered across his mind. He squeezed his brows together trying to block out the picture of the gauntlet and the sounds of agony.

Timothy reached up and put his hand on Henry's shoulder and pressed as if he read his mind as clearly as a page in a book. "Praise the Lord for our deliverance, Mister Clarke. It appears Bezo was the only warrior on either side to survive the Mohawk attack on us. I never would have guessed he would be our liberator."

Olidaha's arms were spread out to the side like the wings of a mother hen's, waving and shooing the children away from the visitors. When she heard her betrothed's name, she dropped her arms and twisted around. Claire was the only one who caught her reaction. She raised her eyebrows as if wondering why such a sweet, young woman would be linked to the barbarous Bezo.

"As ye said," Henry continued, "we are currency— and we are not yet liberated."

"To risk his life like that . . ." Timothy scratched his head, "they may assume we are more valuable than we are. I fear my father does not have the means for a stiff ransom. They may only get what a Frenchman is willing to trade for me, and at present, I am hardly worth one chick. "We cannot rule out that they may even want to keep us to replace those the Mohawks killed." Timothy glanced at Claire. *If the latter proved true, would the Indians separate the Clarkes? They might keep the man and sell the woman.*

Ever since the white man encroached on their land, a

mysterious sickness had claimed the lives of many Indians, a sickness that their herbs and plants proved powerless to combat. Olidaha's family was hit harder than most: She was the lone survivor. Despite the loss of others in the village, the squaws in her longhouse regarded Olidaha with suspicion: Why and how did she survive when her family did not? Some of the squaws feared that she would pass the sickness on to others. They all but shunned her, which only intensified her loss.

Fortunately, Bezo's influence in the community kept her from being ostracized. Whenever he was not on hunting trips, trading with the French or other clans, or on raids, he was always near her, never showing any signs of diminishing health. The squaws slowly commenced to accept Olidaha again; however, when Bezo was absent, she adapted to moving amongst them with little interaction.

The timing of the white people's arrival was mutually beneficial to Olidaha and the colonists. Tomasus put her in charge of the hostages, and in so doing, she became an integral part of a group again, and the trio had a pleasant ally who also administered to their needs. She nursed the men with the special tea and tended to their wounds while showing Claire the ways of their culture. She provided Claire a wrap-around deerskin skirt and a poncho-like blouse with deerskin leggings and moccasins and gave her an animal skin cloak to keep the winter chill away. Perhaps because Bezo had returned to the village, Olidaha had the brashness to convince the squaws to donate a small portion of their food to the hostages until they could manage hunting for food on their own. With help from Olidaha, they did not go hungry.

The squaws were very protective of their positions and possessions around the cooking fires. Claire learned early on which ones were more inclined to nudge her out of the way, grab an implement out of her hand, or ignore her need for help completely. Olidaha often came to her rescue or offered assistance. She had no problem being Claire's intermediary with the other squaws; however, she was not always at Claire's side to do so, and Claire had to fend for herself, with little success, until the women got accustomed to the strange white woman and she became useful.

The squaws eventually began to tolerate Claire, who first earned acceptance with the babies' mothers. She helped by changing diapers with the moss-lined blankets and carried the little ones in a cradleboard on her back, so the mothers would not have to hang them in their frames on poles while they worked.

Many times a day, especially when the snow drifts kept her inside, Claire had to fight the depressing memories that invaded her mind as suddenly as a snake strike and hurt as much as the bite. Timothy recognized a false cheerfulness in her tone when she shared that she beat the horrific pictures away with her memorized prayers and conjured images of her five-year-old twins. He was amazed when she decided to take an active interest in the children, primarily the babies. *She must have a need to punish herself; she survived and they did not.* Henry, on the other hand, never mentioned the children he had lost. He was locked into his faith and continued on with blinders to the past.

As winter raged on, Henry was the first to notice a sudden decrease in the settlement's population. Most of the warriors had left, with the exception of the elders and a small band required to defend the settlement. Many of the older squaws without young children had disappeared as well. Olidaha was able to explain through a variety of motions and a few English words that her people had gone on a long hunting expedition. The women were included to prepare the meat. Their village was a warm weather settlement for the tribe. The men would stay here longer in the warmer months and hunt closer to home. In winter they had to venture farther to get game.

In the cold months, life moved at a slow pace, and they were often bored. Even in their boredom, the three captives dared not speak of home. They did not know if word had arrived of their captivity or not. Their biggest fear was thinking their families believed they had perished and went on with their lives. If no word of the ransom had reached the Indian village by July, each of the hostages harbored thoughts that their futures could be mighty bleak. They spent the winter being hopeful, in the spring concern started to build, and as the temperature increased, so did their apprehension.

A lookout was always posted on the river in the event a Mohawk canoe or English vessel floated down it. One early spring morning, the three awakened to a confusion of Abenaki scurrying around the center of the settlement like ants disturbed in their nest. They poured out from their longhouses brandishing weapons and with fresh war paint smeared on their faces. The lookout had spotted canoes breaking through the early morning mist, but the Mohawks passed, oblivious that the village existed, and paddled toward their home to the west. When the parade of canoes was safely out of hearing range, the Abenakis formed a circle in the middle of the village. Men banged on different sized drums, and shook corn-filled gourds to the beat. They leapt and danced into the center amid boisterous cheering and Bezo stepped forward to reenact his version of the Mohawk massacre with the rescue of the three colonists. As quickly as it had started, the gaiety suddenly stopped. Bezo must have brought to mind the warriors who had lost their lives. He ended his performance by shouting and punching toward the sky with his fist. The warriors responded in kind. Then they went about their day.

The Clarkes and Timothy adjusted to the rhythm of the settlement. As the warmer winds won their victory over the cold and the spring rains bathed the earth, activity around the village increased. It was on one glorious day, when the sky was the color of blue forget-me-nots with nary a cloud in sight, that Olidaha led Claire by the hand and outside the perimeter of the settlement.

They wound their way along a well-traveled path. Every once in a while, Olidaha would stoop down and point to something growing. "Gud," and she would grab her stomach or place her palm across her forehead. After many forays into the scrubby growth along the river or in the woods, Claire began to learn and identify the beneficial plants in the wild and the ones they cultivated. Each one of these had a use, either for food, medicine, dye, or weaving. Claire learned quickly and Olidaha began to call her Wawôndam. The two women were often outside together, Olidaha the teacher and Claire her eager pupil. The language was becoming less of an obstacle and they enjoyed each other's company, unless Bezo was around.

When the oak leaves turned as large as a mouse's ear, the women claimed their garden plots and planted their seeds. Tomasus allowed Wawôndam to plant a small garden and Olidaha shared her seeds with her. She instructed her new friend on their system: Olidaha made small hills, in each hill she buried a fish. She then planted four corn seeds on the top of each hill toward the four directions: north, south, east, and west. Four bean seeds were planted between the corn and four squash seeds were planted around the base of each hill. The beans would climb up the corn stalks, and the leaves of the squash helped keep moisture in the ground and weeds out. They also planted herbs, flowers, and sweetgrass that they dried and wove into baskets and mats. Everything they planted was dried and meant to last the winter. Only the men planted and tended to the sacred crop, tobacco. Tobacco was used in their ceremonies, and the women were forbidden to touch it. It was one of the few responsibilities the men had around the camp.

As Olidaha's sisterly affection for Claire grew, so did her affection for Timothy. He would have liked to return her stares and attention, however, when Bezo was in the village, his presence reminded Timothy that Olidaha was promised to the warrior. Bezo sensed a bond forming and often glared at Timothy as he yanked Olidaha away. Then he found tasks for Timothy to do: the fence, a longhouse, wigwam, or hut needed repairs. Timothy would see Bezo speaking with a squaw and she would immediately order Timothy to do something: bring firewood inside or carry heavy buckets of water.

"Best be aware of any intentions you may have, friend," Henry said with a flick of his head toward Bezo one day. "He is not one to look for an excuse to exercise his tomahawk, especially on you. Do not make it any easier for him."

"If I understood her correctly, Olidaha explained that when Bezo was not much older than Wonkses, his younger brother, white men killed Bezo's father and uncles and left Bezo with the scar as a reminder. As he grew, he developed into the fiercest warrior of their tribe, motivated by hatred for the white man," Claire said.

Olidaha had loved Bezo ever since they were children. As adults, she was privy to the secret side of Bezo. His tenderness toward her was in sharp contrast to the fierce warrior everyone else knew, and it was like a tonic that she readily drank. When it came time to fulfill the Abenaki engagement custom of decorating a box with the virtues of the other, she filled it with a knotted rope for strength, a bone from a bear he had killed, and sweet, delicate flowers. But she was not a foolish woman; she knew about his brutal side. It was what made him a good warrior.

Timothy discovered that when he ventured across the village, he would often become the leader of a parade of young boys, about twelve or thirteen in age. They recognized a source of amusement when they saw it. He enjoyed their company, mostly because language was not necessary and he delighted in making them laugh. They bent at the waist, laughed out what sounded like insults, and made faces at their new white friend they called Nidokan to coax him into chasing them, and much to their delight, Timothy would stop, put hands on hips, and bellow. Then he would rush after the boys, scattering them throughout the village. They were too nimble to catch, so he resorted to lunging at them, which then left him sprawled out on the ground like a squashed bug. When exhaustion overcame him, he growled and staggered like a bear on two feet with his arms outstretched, sending the boys and Olidaha, who was often present, into gales of laughter.

Timothy's favorite was Bezo's brother, Wonkses, who would entertain the others with imitations of Timothy; even the older Indians stopped what they were doing to enjoy the merriment. Wonkses, with the same lopsided grin as his brother's, ears that stuck out like grips on a basket, and comical contortions of his face, often set off chain reactions of giggling that were hard to stop. Bezo was the only one not affected: He often interrupted any interaction his younger brother was enjoying with Timothy with another chore or errand for him to do.

Spring bled into summer. It soon became clear that this year's summer temperatures were unseasonably high. The relentless, oppressive days strung together, one after another. The male Indians' custom was to escape the harsh sun and humidity and spend the afternoons resting in their longhouses, only to exert themselves when it was unavoidable, which it often was not. The three colonists appreciated the custom and willingly complied.

"At home the chores are never done; here it is commonplace for all to work together and only in the mornings and at dusk. This way of life is not hard to get accustomed to," Henry joked to his wife.

"You are speaking from the men's prospective, Husband. The only chores I am aware of the men doing are fishing, hunting, and trapping! Do you not see that the women do most of the work?" Even so, life for both sexes seemed easier. The women were always busy, but happy.

Timothy was resting on his back on his platform, lazily drawing a tree with his finger, when Olidaha entered the longhouse. When her eyes adjusted to the light and focused on Timothy, her face brightened. Timothy, like his friends, typically spoke to Olidaha as if she understood every word he said.

"Too hot today," he said, hoping she would join them. "I fear I grow rather bored. Perhaps you could instruct us on more Abenaki words."

"Words?" she repeated and looked at Claire.

"Yes," Claire smiled and sat up. "This is a good opportunity to learn some more *words*." She looked around the immediate area, searching for something useful to know. She pointed to the cooking area, "Ah, what is . . . fire?"

"Far?"

"Fi-*your*," Claire repeated.

Henry laughed, "'Tis fine! *Far*. What is . . . *far?* He rolled off his platform and stood next to the closest cooking area, the fire long-extinguished when the heat wave made it unbearable to use. He pointed to a blackened log and mimicked getting burned. Then he pointed to his arm where the Mohawk squaw had left a reminder of the nightmare on his skin. "Fire, aaw!"

"Far . . . skweda, skweda, yes?"

"Skwuhdah," they repeated. Now it was Olidaha's turn to laugh.

The vocabulary lesson for the three continued, but the girl's eyes rested on Timothy longer. With her head slightly bowed and her brown eyes peering from under her long, dark eyelashes, she transmitted a tenderness that made Timothy clear his throat, his cheeks aflame. He did not react this way to the girls at home.

⟫⟫⟫⟪⟪⟪

Early on, Tomasus had charged a handful of Abenakis to observe the colonists. When they determined Henry and Timothy were not exhibiting any sign of fleeing, the Indians trusted them with weapons to join them on their summer hunting excursions. If the white men dared to harm anyone or make an escape on such a trip, the expert trackers would have no problem locating them, and the two men knew it. They also knew the punishment would be severe. It helped that the Indians preferred having the white men hunt for their own food; the natives did not like to share their bounty. Soon, the two white men learned to hunt at certain phases of the moon or before a certain height of the sun.

It was now customary for Timothy and Henry to leave early every day with the Indians to hunt or fish, and they often returned with something for dinner. Sometimes, they were lucky enough to bring back an animal substantial enough for the three to have a feast, but mostly their meals consisted of fish or a squirrel and whatever Claire was able to forage or harvest from her little garden.

"I pray we do not have French masters, I am getting accustomed to this lifestyle," Timothy nudged Henry while setting fish traps one day.

Henry smiled. "Indeed, I conclude that perhaps this is a better arrangement. The French would be wanting to get their money's worth out of us and more. They would endeavor to keep us longer. I sincerely doubt we would be permitted to march off into the woods to hunt or disappear down a river to fish as we do here. Our work would no doubt be a great deal harder under a Frenchman's roof."

Timothy pulled up a trap basket and winked at Henry when he saw the fish flopping inside. He pulled the slippery smallmouth bass out and thanked it, as the Indians had taught them to do, before dispatching a quick blow to its head.

Timothy knew his perceived deadline was up for word to arrive from home. He vacillated between hope and despair. "True . . . and the Indians may feel we can bring a better price from home than the French are willing to pay or trade for us, but we may never return if we cannot secure the ransom and the French get us or they decide to keep us, Henry." Timothy had dropped the formality of addressing Henry with "Mister" shortly after arriving at the village. They had gone through too much to be so formal, but he kept the "mistress" with Claire out of respect. On rare occasions, he called her Wawôndam, but only in front of Olidaha. "My father is not a man of means. Where will your ransom come from do you suppose?

"The church may take up a collection when the Indian messengers get to them. It will take time. That is what happened with the Deerfield survivors. I pray someone gets word to our community soon. We, Claire especially, must see our children. Our twins need to know we shall return. I frequently catch Claire with that distant look and struggling to hold back from weeping."

⋙⋘

The blistering late summer air was still heavy. It was like walking through hanging sheets of gauze. Claire was horrified to see the older male Indians walking about without a stitch of clothing on except their moccasins.

"I have just gotten accustomed to seeing the younger men wearing their breechcloths which barely hide their nakedness, but this is too much to abide!" She muttered out loud. "Praise be that the male Indians do not interact with me!" When an offending Indian came too close, she dashed into the longhouse to escape the unsettling sight.

Henry was inside looking for his bow and quiver of arrows when Claire darted in and stopped. Her hand was covering her eyes and she shook her head to expel the image. She looked up to see her husband laughing at her.

"May I never see such a sight like that again! Husband, I pray you will never become so conditioned to your surroundings that you would dare to wear those flaps, those . . . breechcloths! God have mercy if you should *not* even wear *them*!"

"Perhaps we can bring this style back to Haverhill with us, dear. 'Tis a lot more comfortable to get air circulating all around the body," he laughed.

"Well, I am well-pleased that Mr. Corliss's burn is healed enough so he can now wear breeches instead of that flimsy tunic."

"Yes, I suppose that is the only reason he is pleased his injury has improved! He knew you wanted breeches on him!"

A Turn of Events

The next day, just before dawn, as was the Abenaki custom, Timothy, Henry, and the male Indians, including the young boys, gathered their bows and arrows, tomahawks, and knives to go hunting: Their weapons of choice did not make loud noises that would scare away other game. Bezo led the party through the humid forest. Timothy and Henry carried the bows and arrows Olidaha had borrowed for them, and Wonkses toted his bag of darts and blow gun to shoot squirrels and rabbits. With good fortune, they all would return with plenty of meat before the heat of the day grew more oppressive.

Timothy was already wiping a layer of sweat from his brow. Above him the pines were murmuring, but the gentle breeze stayed too high to be beneficial. Perhaps he was reacting to more than the humidity: He was eager to return with a substantial dinner and to save face in front of Wonkses and the other boys. The Indians revered a good hunter; a bad hunter was the object of scorn.

For forty minutes they threaded through the trees barely making a sound. Timothy identified the lively chorus from above as coming from male nuthatches, titmice, and chickadees, warning other males to stay away from their territory. He brushed the insidious gnats from his eyes and ears, but they returned with a vengeance. *I should have covered myself with bear grease.*

The scent of pine gave way to the fetid smell of decaying vegetation and rotting deadwood. The scent hung in the humid air. A blue haze spread over the swampy area. Dead, black-trunked trees, slanting at different angles, were reduced to stick figures, their naked reflections emphasizing their decrepit condition while their robust, verdant kin loomed behind them. An eerie whistling wafted across the skeleton-tree swamp and then whooshed through the tall wild rye grass growing in dense tufts.

The hunters stretched around the eastern edge of the swampy forest, backing away from the intended, invisible outer boundary so no one would be in the line of fire. They maintained enough of a distance to remain undetected by animal life but close enough to hit a target with an arrow. The Indians were not the only ones that preferred to hunt around dawn in this spot. Timothy and Henry identified enough tracks that indicated several prey of theirs would be preoccupied doing their own hunting, making the game easier to shoot.

Henry left to relieve himself as the swaying

branches of a graceful willow tree on the western side of the murky water caught Timothy's attention. *Willow bark steeped in water had eased his pain from the wretched gauntlet. It would not hurt to collect a little bark before we get settled. It could serve a purpose if we encounter any accidents.*

It was as if the willow's branches beckoned to Timothy. *I can quickly cross the outer boundary, scrape some bark into my leather pouch, and within minutes rejoin the party.* Timothy unsheathed the hunting knife an elder had lent him. He walked toward the tree; the tall, waxy stems of the swamp grass brushed against his shoulders. His head was down to focus in the slushy mud where a Massasauga rattlesnake could be lurking. *One bite could save father from having to pay a ransom.* He arrived at the tree without encountering any snakes, parted the long, feathery filaments, and ducked inside the branches. The willow bark was rough and had protruding ridges easy to scrape. He let out a satisfied grunt when his pouch was full. He was about to part the stringy willow boughs again, but he froze. *What was that noise in the tall grass? An animal or just the wind? Was something moving near this tree?*

Meanwhile, Wonkses had seen the V formation ripples and knew a beaver or muskrat was swimming toward the swamp's edge. He was patient. He waited for the thick-furred animal to emerge and become interested in a cattail. He readied his weapon.

In slow motion, Timothy sheathed his knife, removed the bow from his shoulder, and withdrew an arrow from the quiver slung over his back. With the arrow positioned in the bow, he used it to carefully draw aside a willow bough. He squinted. The tiny gnats flew into his eyes and tried to interrupt his concentration. A brownish-red animal about the length of his arm, and within his shooting range, was slinking toward an unsuspecting muskrat dining on a cattail. The predator's white underbelly brushed the ground; its tail was bobbed. *It is going to pounce any second.* He held the arrow with three fingers and stretched the string back to his chin. He raised the bow to look down the shaft at the bobcat. A gnat buzzed in his ear. He released the arrow. As he let it go, he felt his fingers interfere with the release. It was not a clean shot. The arrow missed the target and flew to the left. *Curses on the gnats and no-see-ums!*

In that second, Wonkses loaded his dart and took a deep breath, but the puff of air he expelled did not have enough force to propel the dart. A searing pain had startled him. He snapped his head to the side and stared open-mouthed at the arrow protruding from his shoulder.

No one had expected Timothy to cross to the western edge of the swamp or disappear into the willow. No one noticed Wonkses follow the muskrat until Henry and an older Indian saw him preparing to shoot. Suddenly, an arrow seemed to come out of nowhere. The old Indian said the word that made Henry's knees buckle: "*Mohawks!*" Henry folded and splayed out on the ground, the reedy growth his only protection. When he noticed that others did not react to any threat, he slowly stood up again, more puzzled than before.

Timothy ran to Wonkses's side. The early training an Indian boy gets from his elders is to show victory over pain. The boy looked suspended in time, like a statue. His chin was raised high, and his chest was full of air as if he was not going to exhale. His arm hung limply at his side, the arrow embedded in it. Then, his shallow, ragged inhalations and exhalations betrayed his suffering.

The Indians abandoned their hunting positions. Bezo yelled to them, then took giant leaps across the shortest distance to his brother; his arms circling like the vanes in a windmill as he splashed through the dingy water. A blue heron barely flapped out of his way. The other Indians scattered. Before reaching Wonkses, Bezo ran at Timothy. Without stopping, he raised his bent arm back and with great strength shoved Timothy. The force sent him reeling backward and splashing into the organic matter.

Without uttering a word, Bezo carried Wonkses to drier ground and placed him on his side, so as not to disturb the arrow. He gently tried to twist the shaft; Wonkses, stone-faced, winced but he didn't cry out. The shaft did not move. Bezo blinked at his brother; the arrowhead might be lodged in the bone. If he tried to pull it out of the bone, the sinews, attaching the arrowhead to the shaft, could loosen and detach from the shaft, leaving the arrowhead lodged in his arm. If it remained secured, the arrowhead's sharp edges would tear away at more tissue. If he tried to push the arrow through Wonkses's arm, he would most likely break the shaft and the bone as well.

Bezo shouted another command to one of the hunters and nodded in the direction of a maple tree. The brothers waited while the men scavenged around, seeking materials that could ameliorate the situation. An Indian came running with a six-inch-stick from a maple sapling. Bezo put the green stick in Wonkses's mouth, and he clamped his teeth down. Two Indians held him down. Every time Wonkses moved, the arrowhead's rough edges aggravated the injury. Bezo removed his knife and enlarged the entrance wound. Wonkses controlled the scream he was trained to hold back but could not prevent the tendons and muscles stretching and tightening in his neck. Bezo slid his finger down the shaft until he touched the arrowhead. The arrow was indeed lodged in the bone.

The hunters joined them with wool of the rattlesnake reed, spiders' webs, oak leaves, and prince's pine to staunch the bleeding. The old Indian stood over Wonkses holding stalks of goldenrod. Bezo wasted no time grabbing everything, balling them into a mound, and placing the material around the arrow to absorb blood as much as prevent the arrow from moving. There was no time to find moss and squeeze it dry. He pressed the mass hard against Wonkses's arm. The boy responded by squeezing his eyelids together and breathing rapidly. They fashioned a litter from two maple branches with Timothy's poncho and carried

Wonkses home with the arrow still protruding from his arm.

Claire and Olidaha looked up from the clay pots they were forming. "They must have encountered great luck to be back so soon," Claire said with a smile, but Olidaha wrinkled her brow and bit her bottom lip. With wet clay not entirely wiped from their hands, they joined the other curious squaws to greet the hunters. Olidaha's concerned appearance surprised Claire. She craned her head around the women in front of her to locate Henry and Timothy. Finally, she spotted Henry following way behind the downcast hunters who had already joined family members. Olidaha frowned: No one was carrying any game.

"What have you brought me for our dinner, Husband?" Something was amiss, but she smiled at Henry, hoping she was wrong. He was unnaturally silent. Her eyes darted up and down the line of men, but she did not see Timothy.

Expressions of anger floated in the air as the hunters explained to the others what had happened to Wonkses. Eventually, they dispersed into their longhouses or picked up trap baskets and nets to head to the river. The sun, hiding behind thickening clouds, was too high in the day to go back hunting.

Olidaha had gripped her sides as she heard bits and pieces of the conversations. Wonkses would be her brother when she and Bezo united, but concern for the lad mixed with fear for Timothy. She looked at Henry who had started to explain to Claire.

"Timothy may be over a barrel, Wife. It is uncertain what Tomasus will do with him. Bezo took our friend to the sachem after taking Wonkses to his mother. Timothy shot him with an arrow, by accident to be sure, but it was foolhardy. They cannot remove the arrow without injuring him more. I do not yet know what they will decide to do, but if they cannot remove it, or if the wound festers, they will have to take his arm."

Timothy and Bezo stood in front of the cross-legged sachem. Timothy shot a glance at Bezo. His scar was more ragged and pronounced from the side. Hoping not to sound like he was begging, Timothy repeated multiple times how sorry he was, that it had been a mistake, that he had no idea Wonkses had followed him. Bezo would not understand the words but, hopefully, the sincerity in his tone. The warrior's demeanor had subdued, but only because he was addressing his sachem. He spoke to Tomasus in measured tones, quite different from the harsh commands he had barked with eyes ablaze when the injury took place. Tomasus absorbed every word without comment. Every once in a while there was a slight movement of his head. *Was he agreeing to*

something or just acknowledging his story? When Bezo stopped speaking, the sachem nodded; Bezo turned to leave, his parting glance at Timothy was a searing indictment. I am as good as dead, Timothy thought.

Tomasus's eyes, narrowed by the crumpled eyelids, studied Timothy as if he were trying to read his mind. The man's lips were like a straight gash across his face. Timothy began to shift his weight from one foot to the other. His deerskin shirt had adhered to his back and beads of sweat united to slide down his temples. Finally, the sachem broke the silence.

"Nidokan, it is decided. The General Council will meet with the dawn of the new sun. Go to your longhouse, stay inside, and wait."

Henry and Claire were waiting outside and visible to Timothy before he ducked through the doorway. Claire's eyebrows pushed up to form small furrows in her forehead; she was rubbing her hands under her chin, like she did when fighting the cold many months ago, but it was far from cold. Henry was frowning. They both had their heads cocked, ready to hear Timothy's fate.

"The General Council meets tomorrow morning. I am to stay in our longhouse and wait—I cannot fathom at this time if 'tis a good situation or not for me. I suppose 'tis better than having to fight Bezo. Have ye seen the boy? I should like to go to him. I would never wish him harm. 'Twas a most unfortunate accident. Ye both know I am quite fond of the lad."

Both nodded in assurance, but Henry said,

"Perhaps 'tis not a good idea. Did not Tomasus instruct you to go to the longhouse? We can check on him and advise you on his condition."

Henry and Claire went to Wonkses's longhouse. A squaw stood in the doorway, filling up the space. At first Henry thought she did not see them, but she put her hand up to hold them back in the event they got too close. Claire tried the few words she knew to ask about the boy, but they either were unintelligible or the squaw was reluctant to divulge any information. The downturned corners of her mouth and the stare that seemed to bore through them told the Clarkes there was nothing they could tell their friend.

Timothy rolled onto his side and propped himself up on his elbow. His thumb and index finger on his left hand rubbed circles against his eyelids. His heart's rapid beat and the image of Wonkses, stoic and still as a statue with an arrow sticking out of his arm, interfered with his sleep. His mind darted like a weasel out of a chicken house: *The Abenaki are not known to torture their captives like the Mohawks, but they are vengeful; Bezo demonstrated many times on the trail that he has a mean streak, and his little brother is too important for him to ignore my folly; if the boy dies, death seems evident. Even so, I should delight in Bezo's anguish! He murdered Edward and perhaps was the one who killed the Clarkes' two children! Such cruelty! But . . . I do not wish Wonkses to die!* His mind continued flashing images and presenting worrisome outcomes until at last, the sun conquered the darkness.

"Henry! Wake up. Please, wake up. Go see to the boy. I must know if he lives." The urgency in his voice was louder than he wanted it to be.

"Pray tell, what time do you imagine it is?"

"They shall be meeting soon. The sun is rising."

Henry let a groan escape as if he suddenly realized he had not dreamt the awful accident. He rubbed his eyes and swung his legs over his platform. Claire bolted up and he rubbed her back. "Stay here, I shall return after I see to Wonkses."

Timothy stood in the doorway raking his fingers through his hair and pulling out the knots. *What is taking him so long? Either the boy is dead or alive!* A few Indians came out of longhouses and were walking together toward the meeting and ceremonial house. He held up a balled knot of hair, released it, and watched it float off. *I pray to keep the rest attached to my head and not dangling from Bezo's belt.*

Henry popped out of Wonkses's dwelling and started jogging toward Timothy. He read nothing in Henry's expression.

"The lad has a very rapid breath. He is agitated, but alive. I was shooed out before I could get close. His mother is encouraging him to drink some concoction. His arm is staunched with the same moss they put on us; it appears they have used up a good supply. His arm . . . his arm is gone."

Timothy sat down on his platform and rested his elbows on his knees. His hands raked through his hair again. He thought of the silly games he played with the young boy, his comical grin, and how Wonkses followed him everywhere he went, making him laugh with his imitations. *Oh God, please do not let the boy die.*

Claire was saying something to him about Olidaha. He glanced up and saw the young squaw peering at him over Claire's shoulder. Her eyes were puffy, but they conveyed sympathy that Timothy hoped he deserved.

"I think she said that she could go to see Wonkses for us and perhaps find out more information."

When Olidaha returned, the three English speakers combined their efforts to understand Olidaha's words and pantomiming. It appeared the council had reached some sort of a decision: Nothing would be done until the boy improved—or died.

"She spoke with Wonkses's mother, who said her medicine was not strong enough. He was bothered by belly pain and was behaving like a wild animal," Claire said.

"Dear Lord in Heaven. This is not good news." The Clarkes did not offer any consolation. They exchanged knowing looks: They had seen such signs back home and the end result was always tragic.

The evening grew dark, earlier than usual. "Indeed, a good rainfall would feel pretty fine now," Henry said. He and Timothy were sitting on one of the platforms in front of an opening, taking advantage of any breeze whispering inside. To get their minds off Wonkses, they were discussing the merits of a deadfall trap, while Claire was frying their dinner of parched wheat in bear grease with beans she had harvested earlier. The smell of the sizzling fat wafted over. The aroma would have made them hungry if they were not so concerned for Wonkses. Suddenly, their heads snapped in the direction of the commotion outside.

Bezo and two others stormed into the longhouse, fury in their faces and in the sound of their words. Bezo grabbed Timothy by the arm and yanked him up with such force that Timothy winced and felt his shoulder start to dislocate. Bezo put Timothy in the same hold Atian used months ago by the Peacock River, only this time, Timothy was not taken by surprise. The other Indians in the dwelling stopped what they were doing and crowded around. Tomasus entered, his face was more solemn than ever. "Nidokan, Wonkses's spirit has passed on."

Bezo shoved Timothy out of the dwelling. *How fitting to hear thunder sounding in the distance.* Gusts of wind swirled green leaves down from the trees. The warrior pushed Timothy until they arrived at the long structure they used for drying tobacco. The new crop was yet to be harvested, and the barn was empty.

"Nidokan, you stay here until tomorrow. The council made a decision. Bezo will give you a just death by bow and arrow." Tomasus delivered the sentence as casually as if he was telling them about a hunting party taking place.

Bezo pushed the door open and Timothy slipped inside before giving Bezo another opportunity to push him. Tomasus stationed a man outside the door to guard him and Timothy listened from inside as Bezo's and Tomasus's voices grew weaker; then there was nothing but silence.

Torn Between Two Worlds

*T*he lookout sounded his bird call three times before a warrior finally spilled out of the closest longhouse to join him at his post and analyze what might be a potential threat paddling toward them on the river. Then the warrior, with a smile on his face, descended the rocky path part way to greet the two Abenakis climbing up. By the time the three reached the top, a handful of men were at the lookout's post, eager to alert the village if the bird call meant danger. The two Indians showed them a paper designated for Tomasus; it was well worn from the rigors of the three hundred-mile journey. Correspondence was rare, and the only reason for it this time would have to pertain to the three white people.

Olidaha and Claire were shelling last year's beans in the village center under the protection of an oak tree when the two messengers passed by with the warriors. The children immediately swarmed the men: The messengers sometimes returned with candy or trinkets.

Olidaha strained to hear the conversation, but the men's words tangled with the pleading and questioning of the young ones. Olidaha heard something that made her stand up so fast that she tipped her bowl over and beans peppered the ground. Claire looked at her friend with questioning eyes and a little fear.

"Wawôndam, is good. Is good I think." Olidaha twisted around and ran up to the men. They spoke together for an instant, and then she returned with a more serious expression. Claire stood up.

"What is it, Olidaha?"

"Message from your village. I go to Tomasus now. Quick." She took off again, leaving Claire holding her bowl of beans, a million questions swirling in her mind, and hope flickering in her heart.

Olidaha ran to the sachem's dwelling. She would not be allowed inside, but she could listen just outside the doorway, hidden from view. A light rain pattered on her head and shoulders, but she ignored it.

Claire needed to tell Henry. She wandered around for ten minutes. She attempted the Indian language with a few squaws and felt she had communicated well, but no one had seen Henry. The village is not so big that he can disappear that easily, she thought. The only place she had not investigated was near the hut where Timothy was waiting for his sentence to be carried out. Of course!

Perched on a rock off to the side where the sentry was guarding the hut, with his knees to his chest, head down, and his arms wrapped around his legs, was her wet-looking husband. He looked up, a drop of rain clinging to the tip of his nose. Claire stood in front of him but he could not imagine anything she could say that would cheer him up. He was on the verge of losing yet another friend.

"Olidaha is spying outside the sachem's wigwam. She will bring us news."

The young squaw had walked up and down, trying to look like she was not lingering and eavesdropping on the discussion taking place in Tomasus's wigwam. She had been able to hear quite a lot before an elder discovered her and chased her away. It did not take her long to find the Clarkes.

"The sachem's voice carried on the wind to my ears." She looked at the Clarkes' expectant faces and continued, as best she could in English and drawing pictures in the wet ground. The message had something to do with the ransom. The council would meet today and decide to accept or reject the ransom— just for them, not Nidokan. Henry scrubbed his hand over his face.

"I would say this news should make us joyful, at least hopeful, but I cannot let my spirit sail without all three of us departing this place, Wife."

The air was getting heavy; clouds darkened. The council members from various families in the tribe entered wearing serious expressions that crumpled their leathery skin; they joined Tomasus in the ceremonial building. Their bare feet shuffled slowly to their customary place in the circle; they sat down, the eldest men restraining grunts that sore joints and old war wounds challenged them to utter. Before any serious matters could be discussed, the council began with the customary pipe-smoking; however, their tobacco supply had dwindled to nothing, and the new crop was still in the ground. For the last month, they had to smoke hemlock and ground ivy for want of good tobacco. After the room filled with dancing trails of smoke, they reached the required reverence. Tomasus read the document, written in English, and translated it into their tongue as he went along.

Upon satisfaction of the terms of the ransom and before the ransom is given over, the parties shall be brought to Montreal under protection by the end of August and allowed to board the ship, the Province Galley. For the redemption of Mr. and Mrs. Clarke and children: twenty shillings each, half a bushel of seed corn, tobacco, and five winter coats.

The members of the council debated the merits of the ransom: One elder questioned whether the French would have a better trade for them; another mentioned that the French used to be more eager to buy the white men, and now their trades are not as appealing; another did not like the ransom waiting in Montreal, only to be handed over when the people were on the ship. How can they trust the white men?

Tomasus allowed the debating to go on for over an hour, and then said, "We vote." All elders accepted the ransom. The white couple had been good workers, caused no problems, and the ransom, especially with the tobacco, was better than they would get from the French. Nobody mentioned the children that would not be returning. Tomasus then read the ransom for Timothy.

For the redemption of Timothy Corliss: ten beaver pelts, a jug of brandy, ten shillings, and a pound of tobacco.

The men frowned. One elder raised an eyebrow and straightened his spine. He reminded the sachem that Timothy was to die in the morning. "He is not to be considered!" The others exchanged looks, nodded, and murmured their agreement.

"It is true, he took a life. It is also true you have already said he is to die, but we now have received promise of a good ransom that will be lost to us. Word will get to his people that we took his life the day after the ransom letter arrived. I remind you that the Clarkes will not be returning with their children." Tomasus looked at each member in turn before he added, "Remember, all debates must answer our three truths. Will peace be preserved? Is the decision righteous? Does it preserve the integrity of the clan?" Tomasus paused. "You must agree, and you must be able to answer yes to all three truths."

Thunder cracked overhead and fat drops of rain pelted the roof as the debating went well into the night. Finally they decided that Bezo would have to come before Tomasus. If Bezo agreed that he could answer yes to all three truths, then so be it, Nidokan would pay the price. If Bezo could not justify the three truths with Nidokan's death, the white man would leave the next dawn with his friends.

Olidaha patiently waited for sleep to overcome her, but it did not. Normally, the rain lulled her to sleep, but meddling concerns poked and picked at her, ruining her chance to drift off.

She had grown to love Wawôndam as a sister; they had become inseparable, and she enjoyed teaching her the ways of Abenaki life. At times, however, there was a sadness about Wawôndam that was difficult to penetrate. Olidaha decided that in those times, Wawôndam needed quiet time to work through the sadness. The squaw knew what it felt like to mourn family and Olidaha read the signs in her face. She would miss this new sister that had entered into her life, but if Wawôndam must leave, Olidaha wanted her to leave with happiness, to remember their clan with fondness. If they did not leave with Nidokan, Wawôdam's sorrow would grow and fester.

Nidokan. She was strangely attracted to him, in spite of her affection for Bezo. But Bezo never filled the emptiness she felt for the sisters and parents lost to sickness. Bezo was gone, sometimes weeks at a time, and even when he was in the village, he was often off with the other warriors hunting or fishing. Nidokan made her heart flutter. Bezo never made her laugh like Nidokan.

She gripped her hands to her chest and squeezed her eyes shut. How Nidokan reminded her of her father! Tall, able-bodied and kind. Nidokan's playfulness came to mind and she smiled. Her eyes opened wide when she thought of how Nidokan's people would seek revenge and more Indians would die. She imagined a big war with the French and English coming to fight on their land. The only way to prevent Claire's sadness and perhaps a war was for her to convince Bezo to release Nidokan. She could not bear to see him die.

Scowling warriors surrounded Bezo and echoed his harsh words as he sought support against the white man. A sense of hatred infiltrated the heaviness of the humidity. If any bond had formed between the white man and the Indians, it was washed away as a wave erases footprints in the sand. Even the young boys, who once were eager to follow Timothy around like he was the Pied Piper, were demanding justice for the death of their entertaining friend with the infectious laugh. For them, there was no excuse, no credible justification that permitted any grasp of Nidokan's innocence. Wonkses would never become a warrior or walk the ground again, and Nidokan was the reason.

Olidaha stood where Bezo could see her; he stopped speaking and parted the men with his arms. He wore his long black hair tied in the back now to declare he had found his mate. After the betrothal ceremony, he would shave all around the plait as an outward sign of unity with Olidaha. The grim twist of her mouth and grave expression were signs that she was going to address the decision about Nidokan.

"It is not Olidaha's place to have an opinion. A warrior's decision is final." Bezo scowled.

"Bezo, you are a fierce warrior. Wonkses looked up to you. If he were here, he would say that he wanted to be just like you. You have brought so much honor into our village, and your brother was very proud of you. Wonkses's spirit walks among us; I feel him here. Can't you feel him asking to spare Nidokan's life?"

Olidaha paused; Bezo was firmly planted. He stared above her head, but she continued. "Nidokan was his friend. He gave him the name of Big Brother as a way of honoring both of you."

Bezo stood with his arms crossed and his stance wide, but his eyes lowered to look at Olidaha. She thought she saw a flicker of pain melt into understanding, so she pressed on, her words measured, controlled, like the sachem when he spoke with his council members. "Is it honorable to take Nidokan's life when Wonkses also made the mistake of crossing the outer hunting line?" Bezo dropped his glance to the ground.

"Where does it end, Bezo? Will Nidokan's death preserve peace? The French are at war with the English—if the English come to our land, the French will get involved, then a war will be fought on our land and the remainder of our clan could be wiped out."

Olidaha saw the muscles in Bezo's face relaxing. He remained silent and made no effort to argue or move away. Later, she would regret not ending here.

"You killed Nidokan's friend on the trail and Wawôndam's children . . ." Bezo jerked his head up and drilled his eyes into hers.

"Enough, squaw! You have no right to judge what had to be done on the trail. It was *merciful* to take those who could not survive on their own! Was the white man merciful to my father and uncles? The white man has slaughtered us and pushed us off our land. Now, justice is needed for the one who took my brother from me!"

Bezo slapped his arm against his thigh, swooped up his tomahawk, and stormed toward the forest. The other warriors, standing on the periphery of the discourse, gathered their weapons and followed him; the hunting would not be good at this time of day, but they meant to support Bezo and demonstrate their approval. If Bezo had changed his mind, they would have lost respect for him.

Olidaha bit her bottom lip. Convincing Bezo to alter his decision was a long shot; she was not surprised by his reaction. She let out a deep sigh and directed herself back to the longhouse where she hoped to find Wawôndam. Her bare feet avoided puddles as her mind wandered. She kicked the occasional stone with the same determination she had when playing with her sisters long ago. Until now, she had never thought of criticizing Bezo's actions or defying him.

The Clarkes' enthusiasm for leaving the settlement was tinged with regret for having to depart without Timothy. Even so, they went to Tomasus to say good-bye and sought out each member of the council to nod their farewell. They would be leaving with the next dawn's first light. Timothy urged them to go before his sentence was carried out. They did not have many belongings to gather for the return trip, basically the clothes on their backs; they had borrowed everything else. They were headed to the longhouse when they saw Olidaha, head down and deep in thought, heading in the same direction. It would be difficult saying farewell to her.

Olidaha raised her head to see the Clarkes approaching. Their knitted brows spoke of the sadness they felt. She spun a full circle around to determine that no one was within hearing distance and flashed a big grin at her friends. The sudden display of joy in this less-than-joyous time caused both to make a simultaneous, slight head jerk. Olidaha clutched each one by the shoulder and rattled on in her tongue. Claire shook her head, "Olidaha, slow down. We do not understand."

The young woman did her best to communicate with the English she knew, signing what she didn't, and once again, drawing in the earth. The plan would be difficult, but not impossible; however, if caught, each would face a severe punishment. She did not tell them her punishment would be worse.

The two women tried to walk casually to the longhouse, not to appear conspiratorial, while Henry waited for his cue outside. He did his best to look inconspicuous by searching for a long stick and then sharpening it.

Olidaha, like thousands of squaws before her, had learned the difference between nature's edible plants and similar-looking harmful plants. As a young child, she could tell the difference between what she could pick and what she must avoid. There were two plants growing along the river that resembled each other but had very different effects on the body: wild grapes and moonseed, a poison that often resulted in death. Nevertheless, squaws knew to harvest parts of the Canadian moonseed plant to use as a laxative. The trick for Olidaha was to make a potent laxative without killing the victims, merely rendering them indisposed for a while. She collected sumac berries to give the drink a refreshing tangy taste and deep red color.

The two women went about the task of making the moonseed tea without alerting the other squaws to any suspicious activity. The women were fully engaged in shelling beans, grinding corn, and chattering among themselves. When their tea had cooled, Olidaha grabbed a blanket off her platform and both left with bowls of the tea. Claire took small steps trying not to slosh hers and headed toward the lookout station. Olidaha dropped the blanket off with Henry and waited a couple of minutes before she followed him to the tobacco hut with her bowl of tea. When Henry was close to the hut and saw that he had not been noticed, he dropped the blanket and strolled over to the Indian guard.

Timothy had been walled inside the sweltering tobacco barn for hours. Every inhale peppered his lungs with dust; he coughed and spit out what he managed to dislodge. Brittle bits of dried tobacco leaves adhered to his exposed skin. Sweat trickled down his back and chest. He had long since abandoned the idea of shimmying up one of the posts and trying to break out of one of the ventilation openings. The gap was too small and trying to use his hand to punch out the wood around it while dangling from a post was impossible. The only thing left to do was to contemplate his death. *Would Bezo get the deed done with one arrow or would he look like a damn pin cushion before it was over?*

Voices . . . Henry! He went to the door and pressed his ear against the rough wood. Henry was trying to convince the Indian to let him inside. *The Indian must understand what Henry wants, but he is not responding. Another voice . . . Olidaha.*

Indians charged with duty at stationary posts often received food and drink offerings. Therefore, it was not unusual for someone passing by to donate a hunk of meat or a cool drink to the Indian at the lookout rocks or the one posted at the tobacco hut. The guard did not think anything strange about Olidaha approaching with the bowl of tea. She greeted the Indian and then feigned surprise at seeing Henry. With Olidaha at his side, Henry made another attempt to see Timothy, but the Indian stared off in the distance as if Henry wasn't there.

Timothy frowned when he heard Olidaha's reprimanding tone directed at Henry in her tongue for the benefit of the guard, and then heard Henry storm off.

The prisoner used the back of his hand to wipe the sweat off his brow. He began to breathe faster and adjusted his crouching position to try to hear more. *Could they be concocting something?* He listened to the pleasant sounds of the conversation the guard and Olidaha were having; she did not have harsh words as before—then silence.

He strained to hear anything that would tell him what was transpiring. *Nothing. Olidaha—how could she foresake him?* He thought of her alluring eyes that crinkled at the edges when she smiled. *Did he misinterpret her flirting?* He wasn't all that familiar with the ways of women, but he did not misunderstand her smiling eyes; they transcended any difficulty they had with verbal communication. He leaned his back against the door, stretched his legs out, and heaved a deep sigh. *Wonkses meant a lot to her. She would have been his sister when she and Bezo married.*

The door jerked open. Timothy fell backward. He barely had time to catch himself before the back of his head sloshed in the puddle outside the door. His eyes blinked involuntarily to shut out the rain. He bolted around into a kneeling position and peered up. Henry dashed inside and quickly closed the door, leaving Olidaha to guard outside.

"Henry! How did you . . . where is the guard?"

"Allow me to say he is busy at the moment. We must act fast and make it down to the river before he is able to alert the others. I shall bunch this blanket up to make it look like you are sleeping in the corner. It may afford us a little time. There are very few out in this rain, and if we are fortunate, we actually may be able to get away."

Henry cracked the door and whispered, "Now?" Without turning around, Olidaha nodded. The men began to break into a trot, but she threw her arm out.

"No. Slow. No one notice slow," Olidaha said, barely above a whisper. She cautiously led them to the side, away from the open area and toward the fence that surrounded the village.

As Timothy walked, he felt the welcome coolness of the rain draining the sweat off his face; he licked his lips to moisten his tongue and tasted the salt. A furtive glance behind him showed no one was following them, yet his skin felt prickly. He fought the urge to lunge forward into a full-out gallop. *Someone could jump them from behind at any moment or sound a shrill warning alert.*

"We should separate. The three of us together will cause notice. Timothy, walk close to the fence. Olidaha and I will walk in front of the longhouses."

Olidaha understood and nodded in agreement. Whatever they did, they had to act normal, and normal was usually Olidaha trying to teach them new Abenaki words and learning English ones. If someone saw them walking slowly, speaking to each other as teacher and student, they would not call attention to themselves.

Timothy kept his head down as he followed the fence toward the gate. Sweat mixed with rain dropped off his chin. If he had been a dog, his ears would have been erect and twisting to perceive even the slightest change in sound. He arrived at the gate before the other two. *Where was the lookout? Ah, that's why Claire was not with them.* He stole a glance over his shoulder. No one was following except Henry and Olidaha. He jumped off the small ledge onto the first stone step and gave freedom to his legs. His moccasins slid on the pebbles and he fell on his rear but jumped up again. Nothing was going to stop him now. He raced down the narrow path, kicking up dust and jumping off stones. Two canoes were bobbing in the water. Claire was in the bow of one and holding onto the gunwale of the second. Timothy dashed into the knee-deep water. Welcome splashes cooled his hot torso.

"Hurry! Get in." She looked up and saw Henry charging down the hill with Olidaha right behind. Claire leaned far to the left to try to balance the canoe as Henry flipped himself over the right side. She threw a paddle at him and both dug into the water as Olidaha and Timothy spilled into their canoe.

"I threw all the rest of the paddles in the river. They will not be able to chase us until they find them—and then it shall be too late!" Claire shouted over her shoulder.

Montreal

*P*atches of blue started to filter through the thinning clouds that wind swirled like smoke. The two canoes slid down their way toward Montreal—and freedom. Over and over, Timothy's paddle sliced into the blue water and he pushed it behind him. When he switched paddling sides, water dribbled off his paddle onto his thighs and tickled as it snaked down his legs. He found himself, once again, watching the back of the Indian in front of him and matching her rhythm. This time he smiled; he had great fondness for this particular Indian. Olidaha was present and ready to help them, whatever their needs. They might have nearly starved if she had not intervened with the squaws or taught Claire so much. *Everything was better for us because of her. Dear God! She even saved me from an awful death!* He was anxious to return to his father's farm and get on with the life he knew, but was he feeling conflicted about leaving her? *Would she come with me if I asked?* He spent the next hours contemplating what kind of life they could have together.

Olidaha pointed her paddle at the shore, and Timothy steered the canoe in that direction. *How do the Indians detect where their camps are? The shore was one long stretch of rocks and trees without definition!* As they drew closer, a turtle, grateful for the emerging sun, toppled off a log into the water. Little waves splashed up to the gunwale of the canoe. Timothy swung his legs over the side and eased himself out. Olidaha was already off the opposite side and in the water.

They pulled the canoes out of the river, hoisted them over their heads, and carried them up to a clearing sheltered by tall pines whose branches provided a canopy high above their heads. The ground felt spongy. Pitch and pine needles were sticking to the bottom of their feet. After they put the canoes down, Timothy, bent over with hands still on the canoe, grinned sideways at Henry as if to dare him. The two, being of a like mind, dashed back to the river and pranced into the water until they could dive underneath.

Timothy was the first to pop up. His eyes were closed to block out everything but the cooling sensation and delightful weightlessness. He heaved a contented sigh and floated. Olidaha and Claire splashed up to their knees and laughed as Henry tried to dunk Timothy. The men, unburdened from captivity, played like children.

Olidaha pushed out some nokehick from her belt

and the four of them sat on a boulder, drying in the sun. She held out a chunk to Timothy, who instead of accepting it right away, trained his eyes on hers long enough to make Claire clear her throat. Olidaha lowered her eyes and Timothy took the snack and pressed his lips together to keep from smiling. After finishing their nokehick, Claire poked Henry in his ribs and gestured with a flick of her head to leave the two alone.

An uneasy silence stretched for several moments. The water lapped the exposed rocks along the shore; pebbles rattled and dribbled over each other. Olidaha bowed her head and nibbled her corn cake like a squirrel, appearing deep in thought.

"Come home with me, Olidaha," Timothy said, putting his hand on her knee. "I do not want to say good-bye. You . . ."

"Home?"

"Yes, come with me back to my home. We have a farm, and there is good hunting. You can have a big garden." He picked up her hands and held them between his. She made no move to slide them out, but a pained expression crossed her face. He put his arm around her and they sat in silence.

Claire poked her head around a stately white pine tree. When she determined she would not be interrupting anything, she approached Olidaha. She pointed to the river. "Should we be leaving now?" She pantomimed paddling. There was no response, so she looked at Timothy. He ignored her too. She shrugged her shoulders and turned to get Henry, who had already started carrying one of the canoes down to the water.

A scraping sound brought Timothy out of his thoughts. Henry was struggling with the canoe and trying to navigate around the rocks. Timothy jumped off the boulder, turned to face Olidaha, and helped her down, but he couldn't let go of her. He brought her into his chest and wrapped his arms around her. She circled his waist and buried her face in his shoulder.

Claire and Henry were in their canoe, bobbing up and down with the waves, when Timothy and Olidaha slid theirs into the water. Claire twisted around to get a good look at them and smiled.

For the remainder of the trip up the Iroquois River, Timothy plunged his paddle into the water as if he were trying to stab a fish. He winced as the image of Olidaha's concerned expression came to mind. His shoulder ached from sinking his paddle deep and pushing an excess of water behind him, but the pain felt good. He could think about that instead of the uneasy feeling creeping into his head.

By the time they reached the St. Lawrence River, the sun was hanging low in the western sky. Timothy was too tired to expend any more energy than necessary. His back and shoulders screamed for rest. He steered the canoe around and saw Claire and Henry's canoe far behind. He and Olidaha carried their canoe onto dry land, and Timothy collapsed onto the scrubby weeds growing out of the sand. The young squaw sat down and lifted a lock of hair off Timothy's face. She looked deep into his eyes. Then she brushed her cheek against his. He turned his head and kissed her cheek. He put his hand behind her neck and gently pulled her down to kiss her lips.

Timothy and Olidaha were sitting on the water's edge, side by side, with her head resting on his shoulder and his arm draped around her. Timothy was filtering the sandy dirt through the fingers of his free hand while watching for the Clarkes' canoe; they were about to pass them by when he shouted. Timothy and Olidaha stood on the little beach and waved their arms, as if trying to take flight.

"Is it much farther?" Claire disembarked and picked up a stick to draw the river in the sand. "Could our journey be more than half over?" Olidaha replied with a nod.

"Going down the St. Lawrence shall be a lot easier than paddling up the Iroquois," Henry said.

"Do you think they are following us?" Henry asked.

"Indeed, they shall be worried about losing the ransom. They tolerated us too long to end up with nothing. I suspect we may meet up with them in Montreal. I doubt they will interfere with us before then." Timothy smiled. "It would jeopardize getting their hands on their *treasure*."

The weary four chose the flattest area to rest for the night. They smoothed out the dips and bumps in the stony sand and threw the stones off to the side. Henry was the first to flop down.

"This bed may prove to be as uncomfortable as the numerous ones we slept on during our northward journey, but praise be we do not have to contend with the cold!" Henry said.

Claire was using a pine branch to sweep the stones away. "I simply hope that we shall get enough rest to restore our strength and land in Montreal before Bezo."

Timothy smiled. It would be a good night; Olidaha was nestled in his arms.

"This is the last day I will ever paddle a canoe!" Claire put her hands on her hips, shielded her eyes from the brightness, and looked out on the shimmering water. Her triumphant declaration brought a grin to her husband's face.

"Well, best make haste and get it over with then!"

The four resumed their places in the canoes and stroked into the fast-moving current. They hugged the shoreline and steered clear of the usual hazards: floating branches, rocks breaking the water's surface, and the trees leaning out over the water. The person in the bow kept a sharp eye out for rocks hiding just beneath the surface and rapids too dangerous to take: The current made it difficult to make last-minute decisions.

With the current moving in their favor, they reached Montreal by midday. They hoisted the canoes out of the rocky, reedy water in a small cove protected by a finger-shaped peninsula. The location was not too close to the harbor; they could conceal their crafts in the underbrush and then go by foot.

Olidaha had selected the ideal spot, but would Bezo choose the same one? Timothy shook his head; he was always on guard about Bezo, but it would not matter a pickle if he ended up in the same inlet. As long as they reached the ship before him. *Oh God in Heaven, please Province Galley, please be there.*

Henry began to direct the others up the steep embankment but then hesitated. His abrupt halt sent stones and pebbles cascading down the dirt in a miniature avalanche.

"You do realize, do you not, that the French would just as soon enslave us as look us in the eyes?"

"Indeed," Timothy said, "Olidaha and Claire should wait here. Also, if Bezo is near, he shall be looking for four people. Alone, Henry and I may attract less attention. We shall make inquiries about the *Province Galley*." Olidaha cocked her head and looked at Claire, but Claire just nodded. The two men did not hear any objections and resumed climbing the embankment as Timothy said over his shoulder, "The ship should be here by now," and then added in a whisper, "or perhaps has come and gone."

"Keep your eyes open and your wits about ye!" Claire called out.

The fortified city loomed strong and silent in the distance while the harbor was bustling with chaotic activity. Seagulls swooped down to try to find tidbits of food to snatch. Children scared them back to the sky, running at them, laughing and imitating their piercing caws. Peddlers yelled out their wares. Soldiers in chestnut-brown uniforms lined the docks. The wind knocked one soldier's black broad-brimmed, two-corner hat off his head, much to the delight of the shrieking young boys. The lad was lucky enough to grab the hat before the soldier got to it and strutted around wearing the points facing the wrong way to make fun of him. Indians mingled with the French populace, and fur trappers, staggering under the weight of packaged pelts, stomped on the docks while shouting nasally sounds that danced up and down in their re-criminations. Beggars pulled at Henry's and Timothy's clothing while speaking the strange-sounding language interspersed with English.

Small boats tethered along the docks bobbed up and down. A few were caught under the pier and bumped into the wooden pilings. Timothy and Henry concen-trated on the large ship that was docked at the end of the pier. Both men snaked around the clusters of people on the dock until Henry heard a conversation in English.

Two men, outfitted in double-breasted white vests with gold buttons and blue trousers, looked officious enough. One man, who was deep into recounting a story, held a sheaf of papers by his right side and punctuated the air with his left. The other man was listening, with a smile beginning to curl the edges of his mouth as if waiting for the punch line.

"If you will, sir, could you tell us the name of this ship?" Henry asked.

The sailor with the papers frowned at Henry's interruption. He looked down his nose at Timothy and Henry and, upon studying their Indian attire, took a step backward. He grimaced, shook his head, and replied curtly, "*the Province Galley*, arrived as of yesterday. Boarding will begin at eight in the morning." He took a big breath to fuel himself to finish his story.

"Do you have a manifest I could see? We are not at all sure for whom I am looking," Henry said, a little embarrassed.

"Please, sir. My friend and I have spent the past year as captives. We are newly liberated and suspect that there is someone on this ship that will be able to get us home. We . . ." Timothy stopped. Above the din of the activity, he heard someone calling Henry's name. They both twisted around and looked up.

"Mr. Clarke! Mr. Clarke!" A man was cupping his hands around his mouth and leaning over the ship's railing. He took off his hat and waved it frantically back and forth.

Henry's mouth split into a wide grin. "Reverend!"

"Mr. Clarke, I shall come down forthwith!"

Claire sat with one arm around her knees and sifted pebbles and sand through her free hand. She was both perplexed and melancholy with what Olidaha said to her after the men had left and the mysterious wooden box her Indian sister had asked her to keep safe. Claire stared at it, now by her side. She promised not to open it; the box was not for her. Whatever was inside caused Olidaha to tremble and her voice to quiver when she handed it over, and if Claire understood her correctly, there was a sense of fatality or loss to her words.

Olidaha alternated between pacing back and forth near Claire and wading up to her knees to glance upriver.

Claire had never fretted much over her appearance until now. As she stood up, she brushed sand and specks of dirt off her deerskin skirt and combed her fingers through her hair. "I wish I had a cap to tuck in these unruly curls," she muttered. She picked up the box and walked to her canoe. The sand squeezed through her toes, and she felt the sharp edge of a stone under her heel. She kicked the stone away and stood watching Olidaha, whose back was turned to watch for approaching canoes. The young squaw was always lovely. She was the loveliest when she spoke and her eyes smiled. How would she be received back home? Claire sighed and tucked the box into the stern of her canoe. She glanced beyond the embankment to the path leading to the harbor. Thankfully, there were no fine ladies strolling along to make her feel more self-conscious about her appearance.

Her face relaxed. Two familiar figures were walking briskly toward the cove with an older gentleman, trying to keep up. She walked closer to get a better look. He looked familiar. Henry and Timothy hopped down the rough embankment, with arms out for balance, then slid the remaining distance. They were laughing! They scrambled halfway back to guide the gentleman down.

"The men are returning, Olidaha!"

Olidaha scuttled through the silty water toward Timothy. He grinned, took her hand, and introduced her to the reverend. He finished by saying, "I do not know what we would have done without her, Reverend." She gave a perfunctory smile and then glanced back to Timothy.

"Bezo?" Her breathy delivery of the word and stiff posture made him want to put his arm around her, but with the reverend close, he was reminded of the social mores back home. Instead, Timothy stretched out his other hand and pressed his two hands over hers. He saw the anxiousness in her eyes and shook his head, "No, we did not see him." Her shoulders relaxed but she let go and ran back to the water to peer upriver.

"Oh, Reverend Stone, 'tis so fine to see you!" Claire began to shake and her eyes could no longer hold back the months of fear and uncertainty. Sobbing, she slumped to the ground before Henry and the reverend could catch her. She covered her face and said between sniffing, "The Lord answered our prayers."

Henry knelt on the ground and held her to his chest. "The reverend has brought the ransom! Timothy's father spent weeks inquiring about other missing settlers in the area and finally heard about our party."

"Indeed, when the messenger Indians arrived, and we found an interpreter, at long last we heard about your captivity. We proceeded to send word back to the senior Mr. Corliss. When he was able to return to us, we prepared the ransom letters for the Indians to take back. We regret the time it took, but rest assured, ye were never forgotten. Your Abigail and Esther were overjoyed at the news. They had feared the worst. They begged to come with me, and I almost relented, but your sister, Mrs. Clarke, would not hear of it. Your return will finally put smiles on their faces."

Claire wiped her nose and flashed a smile at her husband. It abruptly faded. "Our children, they do not know—"

Henry attempted to move Claire's thoughts in a different direction, "We will see Abigail and Esther in less than two weeks!"

"How sad it will be to tell them about the little ones," she said with wet cheeks. Henry stared at the ground. Now he, as well, could not stifle the pent up anguish he felt for the loss of his innocent babies.

Olidaha cried out. "Bezo!" She pointed to specks of canoes paddling down the river. The settlers squinted in the distance and then glanced at the squaw to see if maybe she had made a mistake, but she returned their looks with a confident nod.

Henry stood up. "Hastily now! We must get back to the ship. We can start to unload the ransom materials onto the dock before Bezo's arrival. He would not attempt to cause trouble with the soldiers and sailors wandering around. Timothy and Olidaha can hide in the ship."

Henry pulled Claire to standing. She swiped at her

wet cheeks, cleared her throat, and both started jogging toward the embankment. Timothy was going backward up the incline; he had one hand gripping Reverend Stone's and the other holding onto a small sapling for balance as he pulled. The poor man grunted and groaned as he tried to find a foothold on the loose stones. Henry pushed from behind, and they finally made the crest of the hill.

Where's Olidaha? Timothy spun around. Olidaha had not followed. He looked back down the incline. She was not moving. How slight and vulnerable she looked. Her long dark hair twisted and caught up in a sudden gust. She pulled the long strands away from her eyes. She was half-turned away from them and looking at their concealed canoes. He called to her. His hand waved, unnoticed. The others waited at the summit; their calling sounded like one person's echo.

"Go ahead. We shall join you in a moment," Timothy said. He was already sliding back down, riding on a wave of dirt and pebbles.

When he reached her, she was studying the undergrowth beyond the canoes. "We must hurry, Olidaha. Bezo will be here! We must be on the ship before he arrives." He grabbed her shoulders, twisted her to face him, and stooped to peer into her eyes. Timothy lifted Olidaha's chin to encourage her to return his look. His gut rolled. Timothy stiffened when he saw the resoluteness in her eyes. *She is not going to return home with me.*

In a firm voice she said, "Bezo find me in your

village. More white people die. I have no home with Nikodan . . ."

"Olidaha, you cannot return to your people. Your people—Bezo, he will—"

"Kill me, if not Nidokan," she finished for him.

Timothy straightened and rubbed his forehead. He frowned and narrowed his eyes at her. "Olidaha, the sacrifice you made for me!" He had only been thinking of himself and his freedom. She was now caught between two worlds, belonging to neither. *Indeed, if she came home with me, Bezo's hatred for white people would only grow. He would come looking for her, and who knows what war he may start in Haverhill? If I took her to settle some place far away, Bezo would take my father's life in retribution . . . and perhaps that of others. And, how could she return to her village and to Bezo after freeing the man who, in Bezo's eyes, stole his brother's life? Her life is in danger now! There is no good solution!*

"Go. Go now, Nidokan. Canoes are closer."

Timothy looked toward the harbor. Henry had doubled back. He shrugged his shoulders and stretched out his arms to question why the two had not followed them. "Is everything all right?"

"If you are asking if life is fair and just—no, it is not!" Timothy yelled to him. He turned back to give Olidaha a half-hearted smile. She was gone. The two canoes were still in their places, but she had disappeared. *Had she delved into the underbrush or run into the water?* Timothy called her name three times; the last time was barely above a whisper.

Confrontation

$\mathcal{T}$imothy was going in circles by the time Henry arrived at his side. "Timothy, we do not have time to spare. Once the Indians arrive, they will remain on the wharf to intercept you until the ship leaves. If you do not get there before them, you may not be able to board without great bother and dire consequences. I know you do not wish to leave Olidaha, but it looks like she has already left you. Come, we need help unloading the ransom materials. Please, come with me now." Henry pulled at his shoulder.

Timothy twisted away and ran one more time down into the water. Small waves lapped the water's edge, wind ruffled the leaves in the bushes, and seagulls cawed, but he neither heard nor saw any sign of the young squaw stealing away. For all his courage enduring a hard wilderness trek, flaming poles thrust at his naked body, and threats to his life, Olidaha's escape shredded his fortitude. He fell to his knees and covered his face with his hands. He tried to hide the tears threatening to spill from his eyes.

Henry grabbed his arm with more conviction, pulled him up, and spun him around toward the water. "Look, the canoes are getting closer. We must hurry!" He slapped him on the back for emphasis. "Think of your father, your home, anything but her. She will be safe. She is a clever girl."

Timothy let out a long, defeated exhale and shook his head to try to dispel his sorrow. He could do nothing about her now. With head bowed, he followed Henry, clenching his teeth and then turning around every few steps to see if perhaps she had changed her mind. By the time they reached the pier, the Reverend Stone was securing their passage on board the *Province Galley*. Henry quickly separated from Timothy to tell the reverend to purchase only three boarding passes while Claire ran up to Timothy.

"The captain has given us permission to spend the night on the ship. Once we board, the Indians will be powerless to stop you." She paused, rose up on her toes, and scanned the area. "Where is Olidaha?"

"She is—not here."

Claire opened her mouth to ask another question, but Timothy turned away and walked toward the ship as if to show a sudden curiosity about it. Claire frowned but then teetered back and forth, peering around the soldiers, vendors, and others for her husband. Everyone's attention was directed to two Indians, advancing with determination up the wharf.

The older Indian wore a long, billowing cape with

a pointed cap adorned with feathers that bobbed with each purposeful step. Tomasus had donned his finery for the intervention. They moved with conviction; they did not slow nor alter their direction in spite of the people in their path. Bezo's scar and fierce expression parted the throng as if a sudden wind blew them apart. A man tripped and fell backward as he yielded the way.

"Timothy! Reverend!" Claire yelled over the din of the maelstrom. "Timothy must board the ship now. Tomasus is here with Bezo!"

"I will not run like a coward." Timothy took a deep breath and walked next to Claire. Henry and the reverend rushed to his side. Timothy locked eyes with Bezo despite the increased thumping at the base of his neck.

Upon reaching his target, Bezo stretched his arm out to grab Timothy's shoulder. Tomasus quickened his step in time to press down on the warrior's arm and prevent the contact. The reverend looked at the warrior's menacing expression with the jagged scar, took a step backward, and blinked rapidly. Claire linked her arm around the reverend's and maneuvered him to the ring of bystanders starting to form. There was little a woman could accomplish in this situation, and the reverend's frightened countenance would not be of any assistance.

Bezo scanned the surrounding area, narrowed his eyes, and scowled. Timothy knew for whom he was searching.

"She is not here. She disappeared just after we arrived." Timothy waited for Tomasus to translate, and then he said, "I do not know where she is. Ye have my word; she is not on the ship, nor anywhere nearby."

Henry took a step forward and announced, "The ransom materials are on the ship. The Reverend Stone over there," Henry pointed to the quivering reverend, "is prepared to make the exchange. He is a powerful man, our sachem, and shall insist all three of us board this ship."

Timothy glanced at the deferential reverend and shot him an insistent look with an encouraging nod, hoping he could act the part of an assertive leader. The Reverend Stone hesitated. Their eyes were upon him, waiting for a response. He jerked his head slightly back as he caught Henry's meaning.

He cleared his throat. Tucking in his chin and lowering his voice, he said with authority, "Indeed. The ship shall sail tomorrow morning with Mister Corliss and Mr. and Mrs. Clarke on it. Their people await their return. If they do not leave together, I shall be forced to . . ."

"There is no doubt that unfortunate events shall transpire," Henry interrupted before the reverend said anything he could not deliver.

Tomasus addressed Bezo and reported the dialogue. As Bezo listened, his eyes tightened and his nostrils flared with each slow, steady breath. When his sachem finished, Bezo crossed his arms on his chest and planted a wide stance. Claire sidestepped away as the two

Indians began to argue. Henry took three steps backward to converse with sailors hovering nearby. The sailors nodded and left to board the ship. Timothy was surprised to see Claire scamper away and down the wharf. He cocked his head and looked at Henry, who had failed to see her disappear into the crowd.

Henry waited for the heated discussion to subside and then announced to Tomasus, "Men are bringing ye the ransom. You will be pleased, Tomasus." As if on cue, the sailors appeared dragging heavy sacks down the gangplank. They heaved them near the reverend and ran back up to retrieve more. The Indians stood silent and erect. In all, it took the sailors three trips each to deposit the goods on the wharf. The last trip left them sweating and coughing to disguise their rapid breathing.

The reverend, keeping in character, stepped forward and removed a leather pouch from inside his waistcoat. He jingled it in front of Tomasus. "There are fifty shillings for the three. Nothing—if ye choose to keep Mr. Corliss," and he snapped his arm behind his back to hide it. His free arm waved over the mass of beaver pelts, seed corn, winter coats, tobacco, and brandy.

Timothy grew uncomfortable. *The reverend is taking his act a bit too far. The Indians will surely object. No matter what prevails for me, they deserve the ransom for the Clarkes.* Timothy's eyebrows arched high as his eyes trailed over to Tomasus to observe his reaction. He held his breath.

The two Indians exchanged looks. Tomasus surprised Timothy by suddenly asking, "Where—is—Olidaha!"

Timothy bit his bottom lip. "As I told you before, I do not know. She would not come with me to the pier and disappeared before I knew it. To be truthful, I wanted her to leave with me. She refused." He hoped they believed him. He waited while this produced more conversation between the two.

Suddenly, Claire was visible breaking through the various clutches of people. She surged forward, breathless, and holding a box in her outstretched hands. She thrust it at Bezo. The two Indians looked back and forth to each other; they seemed to recognize the significance of the box. Between gasps for air, she said, "Olidaha gave me this box to give to Bezo in the event she did not return to the settlement."

Timothy thought he saw a flicker of tenderness in Bezo's surprised eyes and then witnessed a slight slump of the warrior's shoulders. Timothy raised his eyebrows; he knew nothing about this box. Bezo took the wooden engagement box that Olidaha had made for him and held it as if he feared any pressure would break it. After staring at it for a few seconds, he lifted the top. His fingers pushed aside the stone, bear's bone, and knotted rope. His thumb and index finger lifted out the small bouquet of delicate, wild violets, still bright purple and yellow in spite of their brittle, curled petals. It was as though she was there to tell him she knew he was capable of more than vengeance and brutality. Bezo shut the wooden box and ran his hand slowly over the carved etchings that spoke of their story and the union that would never take place. Timothy hoped he would think of it as a peace offering.

Tomasus interrupted Bezo's thoughts. The sachem spoke to the warrior who then took a deep breath, squared his stance, and puffed out his chest. *Was Tomasus angry with Bezo? Is Bezo being defiant?* Timothy's furrowed brow changed to a frown as both Indians burned their eyes into Timothy's and an unsettling silence followed.

Finally, Tomasus spoke, "We cannot question why Olidaha leaves our village now, but she has chosen to leave." He paused. His tone was unwavering and resolute. "But we cannot forget that a life was taken. Wonkses must be replaced by another life. We take Nidokan now." Bezo stepped forward to grab Timothy again, but the Reverend Stone, aware that the heated discourse had attracted more sailors and soldiers, squeezed between them.

The reverend rubbed the back of his neck and grimaced. He swallowed hard and raised his voice but spoke evenly. "Ye say that a life must replace a life taken. What about Mr. McLane? Bezo took his life. Who shall replace Mr. and Mrs. Clarke's children who were murdered? Bezo stole their lives from these good people as well. It appears to me, Chief Tomasus, that you cannot have it both ways."

The Indians offered no justification or even a response of any kind. They remained silent and firmly planted on the wharf as if their moccasins were nailed into the wood. They *are* going to have it both ways Timothy thought.

With his words falling on stubborn ears, the reverend turned to take Claire's and Henry's hands in his own, and with a slight grip and shake, he flashed them an apologetic smile: It was painful for them to believe there would be no retribution for Mr. McLane and their children. He looked back at the Indians. He cleared his throat, and added with all the authority he could muster, "We keep Mr. Corliss, you take the ransom—and that is the end of it."

Tomasus looked at Bezo and said, "We must answer to the Three Abenaki Truths: Do the three lives you stole on the trail preserve peace? Was the slaughter righteous or moral? Does it preserve the integrity of our tribe?" Timothy, Henry, and the Reverend Stone did not understand the words, but Claire discerned enough to be hopeful. She observed Bezo's downward glance to avert Tomasus's stare.

Whether it was the cocking sound of the sailors' guns or that the reverend and Tomasus had convinced Bezo of the injustice, the white men would never be sure. They watched, slack-jawed, in contrast to the proud warrior's clenched jaw, as he silently heaved a sack of beaver pelts over his right shoulder and plodded down the wharf, the wooden box safely clutched to his side.

Henry pushed Timothy toward the gang-plank. "Hurry before they change their minds. Wife, go with Timothy. I shall be up shortly. All is well as long as our friend gets on this ship!" and he gave Timothy another small shove.

Henry and the reverend loaded the remaining sacks onto two pushcarts. Tomasus strolled over to the tobacco sack and inhaled deeply. The reverend jingled the pouch one more time to get his attention and passed it to the solemn chief, who felt its weight. Bezo returned with two other Indians, and they wheeled the carts through the crowd. Tomasus and Bezo followed. Timothy stood at the top of the gangplank and followed the billowing cape until the throng swallowed them up. *We have not departed yet. One more night.*

Timothy had a fitful sleep. Images of Wonkses and Olidaha floated in front of him. He was bound against a tree. He was a porcupine. Bezo released arrow after arrow, an unending supply, but he did not die. Three arrows punctured his heart, and still he did not succumb. Would his father find him much changed? Would his mother fuss over him, cry? Her berry pie. Would they eat well aboard the *Province Galley*? The angry burn on his thigh. Olidaha. A healing touch.

His mind would not stop. He sat up. He was tired but not sleepy. He slipped out of the hammock and climbed up the ladder to the deck, awash with the light from the moon. He hung his arms over the rail, closed his eyes, and filled his lungs with the smell of freedom. Water lapped against the side of the ship. He was happy. He was sad. She was out there someplace. "She will be safe. She is a clever girl." *I hope Henry is right.*

January 1810

" $\mathcal{T}$ here, there, Father. Relax. It is I, Ednah. I am here with you now." She gently stroked the old man's arm. He did not flinch as before. She turned to the doctor, "I think the laudanum is working now."

The old man blinked to focus on the apparition looming beyond his daughter. He squeezed his eyelids together to dispel the figure's disparaging smirk. When he opened them again, the outline blurred. It was as if the figure was made of smoke that twisted and turned, easing the grotesque leer into a gentle face: The grimace became a smile; the wild and hate-filled eyes softened and crinkled at the edges. Smiling eyes. A candle replaced the menacing torch that threatened to burn his thigh again. The diaphanous shape floated toward him. He was not frightened now. The form became clearer; the squaw's outstretched hand reached toward him. Olidaha spoke, and Timothy understood, even though the language contained all the same strange sounds he had heard so very long ago. His lips quivered and tried to hold a smile.

Timothy's clouded eyes slowly moved to his daughter. "Do you see her?" But the words tangled in his throat.

"He is settling now, doctor. That's right, Father. You are safe, I am here with you."

The Indian touched the old man's cheek. Strength flowed into Timothy's body, yet he felt light; the anvil that had endeavored to flatten his chest lifted. He rose from his body as steady and strong as a young man.

"Father?" Ednah leaned across the still, frail frame, inhaled his musty smell, and wept.

Author's Note

Of the nearly 2,000 hostages held by Indians, many escaped or were ransomed and were able to write about or tell their harrowing stories. There is no record that I could find of the experiences Timothy Corliss endured during his year-long captivity. As a result, I infused the ordeals of other kidnap victims from the same general geographical area and time period into Timothy's story and feel he would have experienced many of the same trials. Hannah Duston, Mary Rowlandson, Susannah Willard Johnson, and the Deerfield and Haverhill, Massachusetts survivors left enough detail of their experiences for me to marvel at their tenacity, courage, and endurance in surviving the harshest of environments under the most fearful conditions. Their adventures teach us how the indomitable human spirit endures in unspeakable situations.

While researching this story, I was torn between feeling rage at the barbarous attacks and horrific murders of settlers and sympathy for the merciless treatment of the Indians as they were pushed out of their ancient homelands. The white people decimated the Indian nations with smallpox and measles, making it easy to steal their land and their hunting grounds. It is no wonder the Indians retaliated as their people and world dwindled.

The Abenakis allied with the French, but conflicting information shows the Mohawks as English allies and French allies. I can only guess it is because clans broke off from tribes to settle and hunt in different locations and allied themselves with one or the other nation as required.

After his abduction and after Weare became a settlement, Timothy Corliss and his parents moved near where he was captured. Timothy eventually married and raised nine children, Ednah being one of them. The Clarkes, Olidaha, Bezo, and Wonkses are fictitious. However, a sachem named Tomasus did exist. *The History of Weare 1735–1888* states that after the French and Indian War ended in 1763 Indians roamed freely in the Weare forests without incident but rapidly shrank in numbers as they left to join larger populations in Canada.

Glossary for Timothy Corliss

1. *Sachem*: chief; leader
2. Bezo: fierce; wildcat
3. *Nokehick*: parched corn cakes—provisions the Indians carried when traveling or hunting; they stored them inside cloth or snakeskin belts.
4. *Rod*: 16 ½ feet
5. *Hobbenis*: groundnuts
6. *Namossack kesos*: place of many fish
7. Wigwams: housing for the Northeastern Indian; the permanent dome-shaped structures were constructed with poles, sheets of birchbark, and mud. They were covered with many layers of animal skins, and rope maintained their position. More portable ones were conical in shape.
8. *Olidaha*: kind; often Indian babies were not named right away. The children's character or personality *showed* their names to their clan as they grew.
9. *Wawôndam*: clever
10. *Wonkses*: clever; fox
11. *Nidokan*: older brother
12. *Skweda*: fire
13. *Portage:* carry boats overland from one navigable water to another.

Acknowledgments

This book would never have seen the light of day without William Little and his team who came to Weare, New Hampshire in the 1880s and conducted interviews with the townspeople for *the History of Weare 1735-1888*. They recorded the stories mothers and fathers had repeated for over a century and a half and gifted me the nuggets of information that sparked the ideas to write about Reuben Favor and Timothy Corliss.

After the spark lit the fuse, I leaned heavily on the insightful advice of my husband, Gary, and was encouraged by the generous help of my Weare Area Writers Guild friends: Sharon Czarniack, Marge Burke, Tom Clow, Ellen Reed, Jen Hallock, and Bob Jarvis.

I am indebted to Sandy Methven and Ann and Dick Ludders as well as Gary Evans who generously donated their time and skill as my beta readers. Their keen eyes caught errors and inconsistencies I had overlooked. Brooke Goode boosted my confidence by her commentary after finalizing the endeavor with her editing expertise while Amanda Stacey worked her magic to design an eye-catching, handsome cover.

I would be remiss if I did not thank Native Languages of America for supplying me with the Abenaki names for the characters in *Timothy Corliss: An Indian Hostage.* I sent them descriptions of the people I wanted to use to tell my story, and they sent me back suitable names to fit their personalities and dispositions. The translations are in the Glossary.